T0142575

THE MYSTERY
OF THE
MISSING GOLD

Rick Oates

Order this book online at www.trafford.com
or email orders@trafford.com

Most Trafford titles are also available at major online book retailers.

Printed in the United States of America.

ISBN: 978-1-4669-8005-1 (sc)
ISBN: 978-1-4669-8007-5 (hc)
ISBN: 978-1-4669-8006-8 (e)

Library of Congress Control Number: 2013902361

Trafford rev. 02/11/2013

 www.trafford.com

North America & international
toll-free: 1 888 232 4444 (USA & Canada)
phone: 250 383 6864 ♦ fax: 812 355 4082

Dedicated to my Mom whom I love dearly.

Chapter 1

Crash Aftermath

The hospital administrator at the Lake Tahoe Community Hospital pushed the documents across the desk to Steve. She picked up a pen and pointed to the signature pages.

"Sign here, here, and here."

Steve signed as instructed and pushed the paperwork back to the administrator.

"Sure is a lot of paperwork for a day and a half in the hospital," Steve said.

"Yes, I know, Mr. Mitchell, but these days, we have to cover all our bases. Lawyers and stuff, ya know."

Steve's hospital stay for the superficial injuries he sustained from a canopy-bird impact turned out to be minimal compared to the impact the flight had on his perception of reality. The vintage Curtiss Helldiver warplane he was test-flying brought Steve to a place that seemed so far removed from reality that it shocked his system.

George Masters, the owner of the plane, watched the entire accident take place. Steve was on his final approach for landing when a flock of large Canadian geese hit the canopy, shattering it and raining wreckage on Steve as he was piloting the plane for a landing. George thought for sure Steve was going to crash, but miraculously, he landed wheels down and without further damage to the aircraft.

Even more startling to George was that the canopy gasket had wrapped around Steve's neck, rendering him unconscious during the entire landing process. George could not understand how a more severe crash did not happen.

Steve on the other hand had no recollection of the physical impact. He just remembered seeing a bright light and hearing a high-pitched squeal when he flipped the switch to bring the flaps down. Not until the plane came to a stop on the ground and the rescue workers removed the gasket that was restricting Steve's breathing did he regain consciousness. What took place during the relatively short amount of time he was unconscious is what caused Steve a great amount of perplexity.

During that time of unconsciousness, Steve somehow spent an entire twenty-four-hour period back in the year 1962. He found himself caught up in the middle of a mob-assassination plot to murder the president of the United States.

The last thing Steve remembered during that time was a mob thug attempting to choke him to death. When he came to, he was back in the present day and the rescue workers were removing him from the plane.

It left a lot of questions in Steve's mind about what really happened that day back in 1962. He knew JFK was assassinated in 1963 and Lee Harvey Oswald was accused of being the triggerman. But what became of the plans the mob had back in 1962? He wondered if they succeeded in their payoff manipulation and Oswald was just a pawn in their scheme.

Nonetheless, he now had to find out the truth about what happened that day he spent in 1962. He told his story to only one person, and that was his newfound girlfriend, Julie.

She was his primary nurse during his recovery after he crashed his Cessna 310 airplane back in Minnesota several weeks earlier. Steve and Julie grew close during that time and began dating outside his recovery window. When she heard Steve had once again had a close encounter with a catastrophic accident with a different airplane, she made immediate plans to join him.

Steve was excited to see her show up unexpectedly at the Lake Tahoe Hospital. She was a sweet and caring person. Upon hearing of the accident, she did not hesitate to use her remaining vacation days from her nursing position and head cross-country to be with Steve at his bedside.

While in the hospital, he relayed to Julie his seemingly unbelievable encounter with time travel. It made her hesitant to say the least. Steve's story seemed so far-fetched that it caused her to question her sanity. But she knew firsthand about Steve's history. It would not be the first time he had traveled back in time. Although others would consider his story as nothing but fantasy, she believed what Steve experienced was far from a dream.

Steve had a confidence in Julie that she believed in his encounters. He felt she understood him like no other person. Steve had no reservations in asking Julie to work with him on finding the truth about that day he spent in 1962.

Julie had no second thoughts in accepting his offer of adventure. She knew how her heart felt about him, and nothing would be more pleasing than to be by his side as they sleuthed out the mystery of that day.

Julie informed the hospital back in Minnesota where she worked that the two weeks of vacation she was on would serve as her formal notice of resignation from her nursing position. She had no regrets, and there was no looking back. Julie herself was looking for answers to some troubling experiences in her own life. Steve seemingly gave her the confidence to look beyond her fears and embrace the truth.

While Steve was signing himself out in the administration offices, Julie went to retrieve the rental car she had taken to the hospital. On the way to the parking lot, she briefly questioned her judgment in quitting her nursing position. She had seniority over younger workers, vacation time, and benefits, but the job had become mundane. Steve initially gave her a sense of comfort, and to have the financial freedom to be with him was an opportunity to break free from the doldrums she was experiencing at the hospital.

Julie was second-guessing her decision on her personal quest to find the answers she thought she needed to find. She was moving from her comfort zone into something she might not be prepared to handle emotionally.

Julie pulled the car to the curb. Steve climbed in the passenger seat. He looked at Julie and gave a wink. Julie just smiled. She put the car in drive and headed out of the hospital's parking lot. Both had a lot on their minds. It was the beginning of a new era for the two of them.

Steve Recalls His Story

"So, boss, where we going?" Julie asked.

"Hmmm . . . first, I need a cup of coffee and to think this process through. Head to the main drag through town, and we'll stop somewhere along there."

Julie drove to the edge of town where a local coffee shop was located. She parked the car, then fumbled with her purse, almost spilling its contents to the ground as she stepped from the driver's seat. Steve smiled and rolled his eyes while slightly shaking his head at the spectacle. His gestures made her snicker at her own clumsiness. Steve's sense of humor made her feel comfortable to be around him.

The two of them crossed the parking lot and entered the building. Steve went to the counter to order two coffees while Julie moved to a table in the corner of the lounge area. Once seated, she pulled a pocket-size notepad from her purse. She knew Steve would have a lot to say and thought it would be a good idea to take notes. The experience was all in his mind, but she needed to jot down his activities so she could maybe be helpful in solving his mystery.

Steve paid for the coffee and stood by the corner counter, waiting for the two cups to be made. He thought about his choice in asking Julie to join him in tracking down his experiences. He questioned whether his actions were too quick. After all, he had not given it much thought and asked her almost on a whim. He was accustomed to being alone. He wondered if he was going to feel overwhelmed by having someone with him most of the time.

Steve passed off his thoughts when the coffee was set on the counter. He determined to be unwavering in his decision. He would have to make the best of it no matter the outcome. He took the coffee cups and headed to the corner table where Julie was sitting.

"There ya go, gorgeous."

Steve placed the cup of coffee on the table in front of Julie.

"Let me get you some milk for your coffee."

Julie gave him a stunned look.

"What? What's that look all about?" Steve inquisitively asked.

"How did you know I use milk in my coffee and not a coffee creamer? We've been to dinner several times, but we have never gone for just a cup of coffee."

Steve was dumbfounded.

"I don't know. It's like I just knew. I didn't give it any thought. You see, that is why I want you with me. We have known each other for only a short time, yet we read each other so well. I'll be right back."

Julie sat staring out the window, thinking of his words.

Steve returned and set a small pitcher of milk in front of her coffee. He sat down, leaned back in his chair, and sighed. His mind was filled with so many questions on what he had just experienced.

"Julie . . . Julie . . . Julie, there is so much running through my mind right now. I don't know where to start."

"Well, Steve, think of all you experienced, and what is most important for you to resolve right now?"

Steve rubbed his chin as he thought.

"I would have to say it's the gold. I saw where Billy and Luke buried it. I've got to find out if it's still there."

"Gold, what gold? Billy and Luke? I'm lost. Who are they?" Julie asked.

"Yes, if you are going to be my assistant, I better fill you in on some of the people I talked with and the events that surrounded them. You need to understand what this is all about.

"As you know, I came here to Lake Tahoe to purchase a plane. Next thing I know, it's 1962 and I'm being told I was brought to Lake Tahoe to drop a crate of gold off the coast of California. The gold was to be a payoff from the mob to assassinate the president. Seems this mob organization had some vendetta against the government, and they thought it started with the president.

"I met with a high-ranking crime boss named Jake. He seemed to be running the operation. He was head of a casino called Cal Neva.

"Write that name down so we can research what became of that place. I doubt it's still in operation.

"Anyway, the gold was going to a group of Russians who were hired to assassinate the president. Seems the mob wanted to wash their hands of any perceived involvement in the deal. That's why the Russians were hired.

"Billy and Luke acted as henchmen for Jake and were in charge of getting me to do the gold drop with the plane. They are the ones that masterminded a plot to steal the gold out from underneath Jake's nose. It was quite a bold move."

Julie asked, "You mentioned gold and it being buried somewhere. Tell me more about that."

"Well, I got to the Eureka Airport in California, which was my last check station along the way, and instead of heading out over the coast, I faked an engine malfunction on the plane."

Julie interrupted. "Steve, why didn't you just fly away from these thugs when you got the plane in the air?"

"Sounds easy enough, but they had the plane rigged with explosives. Their ultimate plan was to blow up the plane moments after I did my drop. I guess I was expendable. They also had it rigged to blow up if I got off course. I was stuck. I had to stay on their flight plan. That's why I faked an engine misfire in Eureka. It was my last chance before the plane was blown up in the air."

"What happened when you landed?" Julie asked.

"I was met by a woman named Samantha Thompson. Uh, write that name down too. I need to find out about her and what her real motivation was.

"When I landed, there was no doubt she was obviously involved in the ordeal. She was also pretty shook up with the turn of events—mainly with me having landed the plane at the Eureka Airport.

"I'm not quite sure how the next scenario played out because I was unsure how long it would be before the bomb in the plane detonated. Somehow the Russians ended up blowing up her friends and their boat off the coast of California. That boat was intended to pick up the gold once I made my drop.

"I convinced Samantha that we needed to get the crate of gold out of the belly of the plane in the next few minutes, or everything would be in pieces when the bomb went off. After that is when I discovered the gold was missing from the plane.

"Once I dropped the crate and popped the lid, I discovered the gold had been switched out with sandbags. It was then when I had to start piecing things together to figure out who made the switch of the gold.

"Oh yeah, write this down: *ST MPLS 62.*"

"Okay, Steve, and what does this have to do with your experience?"

"When I first took the plane for a test flight, I saw that etched in the plane's dash. I thought at the time that it was odd that George wouldn't have buffed it out when he restored the aircraft.

"Then when I went back in time and flew the plane on the way to the gold drop, it wasn't there anymore. But in Eureka, while attempting to retrieve the gold from the plane, it mysteriously reappeared—carved in the dash again. The only person in the plane at the time was Samantha. So for some reason, she etched that in the dash."

"Okay, so you're in Eureka . . . the gold is missing . . . some explosion took place off the coast . . . then what?"

Julie was eager to hear the rest of the story. She rigorously jotted notes as Steve continued speaking of his experience in 1962.

"Well, Billy showed up at the airport. Samantha and I quickly hid from sight. Another thug showed up too, and I watched Billy shoot him in the back. He also shot the plane, rendering it useless. He left, and soon after, Samantha and I left too. We followed him to the town of Trinidad, farther up the coast of California. We stopped just out of sight of a local seaside restaurant.

"Samantha dropped me there and said she was going to drive to her home in Minneapolis. She was quite emotional over the whole ordeal.

"Billy was ruthless. While watching him there at the restaurant, I saw another person show up. His name was Luke, and soon afterward, a third person arrived. Billy and Luke beat the life out of that third person, and then the two of them took off.

"It was shortly after they left in a big Lincoln that I figured out Billy and Luke had stolen the gold and it was in their car. I hot-wired the car Billy left behind at the restaurant and followed the two back to the Eureka Airport.

"While there, the two disposed of the body Billy had left behind at the airport earlier and grabbed the wooden crate from the plane. Again, I followed them until they stopped at a roadside motel in the early morning hours. I was tired but forced myself to stay awake to watch what their next move would be. Not long after it appeared they had gone to sleep, I silently slipped closer to the Lincoln they had been driving. My plan was to grab the gold from the trunk and run.

"I broke into the car and managed to pop the trunk open. I quietly grabbed two of the gold bricks and took them back to my car. I was about to go back for more when something must have spooked Billy while he was sleeping. He and Luke came outside with their guns drawn. I tried to run and hide in my car, but he must have gotten a glimpse of my car bumper sticking out from the side of the building. Billy had to have recognized it as the car he left back in Trinidad. Once I knew I had been spotted, I started the car and took off down the road. Billy and

Luke were following close behind, trying to run me down. Billy's gun was blazing the entire time, and his aim was for me.

"Fortunately, I outran them and circled back behind their Lincoln. I found them at a café, having breakfast a couple hours later. They left the car unlocked, and I wrote a note exposing Billy and Luke as the thieves that stole the gold. I took the note and a single brick of gold I had and hid it in the empty crate that was in the backseat of their car.

"My hope was that Billy and Luke would try to use what they thought was an empty crate to get the heat off them while answering to Jake. If it worked out as I planned, Jake would find the brick of gold and my note incriminating Billy and Luke.

"From there, I followed them to a location off the main highway where they pulled back in the woods out of sight from the rest of the traffic. While I was there, I witnessed them bury the remainder of the gold. They dug a hole and placed the gold in it. They then marked the location by placing an old toilet seat on top of the hole. Billy nailed a Cal Neva Casino coin to a tree a short distance from the hole to also mark the spot.

"After they hid the gold in the woods, I followed them back to the Cal Neva Casino. I parked the car so that I could watch Jake's office. I wanted to make sure my plan of exposing Billy and Luke worked. Well, before long, some thug busted the window and dragged me out. He took me to Jake's office where a fight ensued between Billy and I after Jake had discovered the single gold brick and the incriminating note I had written. Billy had a choke hold on me, and that's when I blacked out and ended up back in the present time."

"Steve, I am amazed at what you witnessed. What seemed like an entire day to you appears to have happened in just a few minutes of time between the bird strike and being rescued. It's so hard to understand. But I do have a question. Do you think the gold is still hidden in the woods?" Julie asked.

"I assume so. I think it would be a wise move on our part to track down that area I saw Billy and Luke bury the gold and see for ourselves if it's still there."

Julie smiled and gathered her things, ready to hit the road.

"Let's not waste any time. Of course, we will need to stop at a hardware store to get a few tools for digging," she said.

Steve told Julie he would drive. Even though the gold was buried years ago, in his mind, it was just like yesterday. He was confident he could retrace his steps to the spot.

He walked to the passenger side and opened the door for Julie to get in the car. Although he was excited to find the gold, he still did not lose his gentleman qualities. He cared about Julie and wanted to remind her of that as often as possible.

They stopped at a local hardware store on the way out of town and purchased a shovel and a pickax. They were ready to do some prospecting. Steve headed the car out of town and toward Route 20 in California. He hoped the three tall pines that marked the edge of the dirt road where the gold was hidden were still visible.

The Mountain Drive

The air was brisk that day as they crossed over the Sierra Nevada Mountains. The leaves had already begun the transformation from summer to fall. The sun shone through the blues, greens, and reds of the hardwood trees, creating a kaleidoscope of color that soothed the senses.

Julie had developed a feeling of adventure once again. It had been years since she felt so alive. To be with Steve on a quest to find hidden gold brought a smile to her heart and her face. She didn't want this day to end.

She turned and asked him about his experience that brought about the riches he now had.

"Steve, when you were, let's say, transported back to the 1860s, you mentioned briefly about being in love with someone. What was that like?"

He did fall in love back then with a schoolteacher named Jean, but to talk about it now was hard for him. The hurt of not being able to bring resolve to that relationship bothered him much more than he cared to talk about.

"Julie, sometimes it's best to let the past be without rehashing the events of a situation. That was a tough time, and if you don't mind, let's not discuss the subject right now."

Julie felt hurt by his answer. She had questions she just wanted answered, but in fairness to Steve, she decided to do just as he asked and not bring the subject up at this time.

They continued driving toward the location Steve saw Billy and Luke bury the gold that day back in 1962. While driving, they speculated on what became of the Cal Neva Casino and its mob owner, Jake. It was a question that would need answering but not at this time. The pressing situation right now was to find that gold.

Chapter 2

The Buried-Gold Site

Steve slowed the car as he made the curve in the highway. He was looking for a dirt road with three tall pine trees on the northwest corner. The undergrowth was much more than when he saw it in 1962, but remarkably, modern progress had not yet attached its tentacles to the area. It had the same wilderness-growth appearance as it had years earlier.

"This might be it," Steve remarked.

"I remember the road making a large sweeping turn to the right. The turn helped me to keep my cover from being discovered by Billy and Luke. I think it's just a little farther."

Steve continued driving ever slowly around the corner. He was looking for those three tall pines.

"There! There they are," Steve excitedly said.

He turned the car down the same dirt road he had in 1962. The forest growth had greatly taken over the path.

"How far back in does this thing go?" Julie asked.

"It goes back quite far. I guess Billy and Luke wanted to make sure no one saw them. One thing is for sure, they didn't see me sneak up on them. See that clump of bushes with what looks like a path going around the left side?"

"Yes," Julie answered.

"That is where I drove off to hide the car. I crept up on them while they were burying the gold. This time, I'm driving right to the spot."

Steve rounded the corner and came to a fairly open clearing with a couple of badly dilapidated buildings set off to one side that once were an old hunting shack and toolshed.

"By the looks of these buildings, it appears this place has been abandoned for quite some time," Julie commented.

"That's a good thing for us," Steve answered.

Steve stopped the car next to what was left of the building. He sat looking in all directions, trying to get his bearings on where the gold was buried.

"Come on," he told Julie as he stepped from the car.

"Before Billy and Luke left here, they nailed a Cal Neva silver medallion to the base of a tree ten paces from where they buried the gold. Start checking the bases of these trees on the right over here. We find that silver medallion, and we hopefully find the gold."

Julie and Steve started checking the bases of each tree. The grass and weeds surrounding the trees were tall, and it made it a little difficult to do a thorough search.

"Steve, I think I found it!"

Steve hurried to the tree where Julie was standing. She had the grass laid flat and pinned under her foot. There at the base of the tree was a silver medallion nailed to the trunk. The Cal Neva logo was still very much visible. The weather elements had not overcome much of the coin's luster. It still shimmered in the sunlight.

Steve went back to the car and retrieved a shovel. He placed the edge of the shovel behind the coin and pried it from the tree. For the most part, the nail holding the coin to the tree had rusted through, and the coin popped easily from the nailhead.

Steve flipped the coin to Julie.

"Hold on to that. It may give us good luck."

Julie slipped the coin in the pocket of her jeans.

Steve placed his back to the tree and walked ten steps toward the shed. It was the same path Luke took years ago to mark where the gold was buried.

"Hmmm."

"What, Steve?" Julie asked.

Steve was busy looking at the ground in all directions.

"It should be right here. I remember they marked it with the lid of an old toilet seat. But I don't see that."

"A toilet seat? I found one lying over there next to that tree," Julie said.

"By the tree? I saw Billy place the lid over the top of the hole to mark where the gold was buried. Evidently, someone has moved it because it wasn't by the tree."

Steve turned to walk toward the lid when he suddenly fell to his knees. The overgrown grass and weeds were covering a hole that Steve did not see.

"Are you okay, Steve?" Julie asked.

"Yeah, I'm fine," he said as he stood and dusted himself off.

Steve pulled back the undergrowth, revealing a hole approximately four feet deep. In the bottom of the hole, mixed with dry leaves and twigs, were cloth remnants. He looked at the hole and made purposeful steps toward the tree where the silver medallion was found. He stepped exactly ten paces.

Steve's enthusiasm began to wane, and frustration was setting in. He realized the empty hole he stumbled in was the same hole where the gold was buried. He was so close to the gold before, and now he had no idea where it had disappeared to.

"Julie, we missed it. That hole is where the gold was buried. Billy and Luke had wrapped it in a sheet, and I see pieces of rotting cloth all over the bottom of that hole. Someone got here before us, and by the looks of the undergrowth and that disintegrated cloth, it was quite some time ago."

Julie, recognizing Steve's frustration, put her arm around him for comfort.

In almost a whisper, she said, "I believe you that the gold was here. I believe you when you said you went back to 1962, and I believe you can find out where this gold went to. You're smart, Steve. Think, where could it have gone? Do you think it ended up going to the mob for a hit on JFK after all?"

Steve stared straight ahead at nothing in particular. His mind was replaying the entire scene of that night he saw Billy and Luke burying the gold. He had come so far and now this. But he knew Julie was right. He wasn't going to let this go. He was determined to get to the bottom of it. Steve knew what he saw, and it was not a dream. The gold was here, but someone had taken it.

He turned, looked at Julie, and said, "I know you're right. I just have to find a way to get to the answers I need. Wow, where to go from here?"

Steve sighed as he thought of what to do. He knew someone had taken the gold but who? *Maybe it was Billy . . . or Luke? Maybe it was even some lucky drifter.* The people and places from the day he spent back in 1962 flooded his mind.

Julie sat down on an old tree stump and watched Steve ponder the present turn of events. She pulled the Cal Neva Casino silver medallion from her pocket and twirled it in her fingers. As Steve thought about what to do next, he noticed the coin in Julie's hand.

"I know where to begin," Steve said.

"It's right there in your hand. We need to retrace my steps to that day I spent in 1962, and the last place I was at then was the Cal Neva Casino. We need to go back to Tahoe and ascertain anything we can about what became of that place. I have a feeling our journey will begin there."

Julie held the coin up to the light and began examining the coin intently front and back.

"See, Steve, this Cal Neva coin already has given us a lead. I'll keep it handy," Julie said as she slipped the coin back in her pocket.

Steve and Julie returned to the car and headed back to the Tahoe area. Their quest was just beginning. Their journey would bring both of them to some very startling revelations. There were some untold stories neither of them were ready for.

Back in Lake Tahoe

Steve pulled into the parking lot next to a scaled-down department store. The streets were filled with tourists from all walks of life. Small shops lined the simple streets. The buildings and the properties surrounding them had the same look and feel as if one developer built the entire four-block complex.

At the corner of one of the buildings stood a sign that read Retail Space for Lease. The name of the property's real estate broker was Chevy Properties. Steve asked Julie to write down the name and phone number listed on the lease sign.

"We need to find out who started this complex. By the looks of the land, I believe this is where the Cal Neva stood," Steve told Julie.

Steve drove down the street, and two buildings away stood a one-story brick office building. The sign out front read Chevy Properties.

Steve looked at Julie and joked, "Nice job on finding the office building that matches that phone number you took down, wouldn't you say?"

Julie just smiled and rolled her eyes.

A Chance Meeting

Steve parked the car in one of the visitor-parking stalls. The brick office building, with its finely manicured lawn, was most impressive. It was clearly evident that no expense was spared in the construction phase of the building.

Steve and Julie entered through the double glass doors and were met by a very attractive receptionist on the phone. She smiled as the two approached the front desk. She politely placed her hand over the telephone mouthpiece and whispered that she would be right with them.

As the receptionist continued with her phone call, Steve and Julie admired the lobby. It was trimmed in rich, dark cherrywood highlighted with large pane windows along three sides. On the west wall hung a group of pictures that caught Steve's eye. It was a chronological view of the construction of the company's building phases. The very first picture captured Steve's attention.

"Look, Julie. There it is."

Steve was pointing to the building in the picture. It was a picture of the old Cal Neva Casino. Seeing the building made Steve apprehensive. His finger shook slightly as he pointed. The subsequent pictures showed the demolishing of the casino and the building of the strip mall that Julie and Steve just visited.

A portrait of a man that appeared to be in his early sixties hung on the wall. The name on the portrait was Thomas Slater. He was an astute-looking individual with short-cropped salt-and-pepper hair.

The receptionist finished her phone call and asked Steve, "May I help you?"

"Yes, you may, and your name is?"

"Barbara," the receptionist answered.

"Hi, Barbara, my name is Steve. This is my assistant, Julie, and we are here to talk with Mr. Slater. Is he available?"

"Is he expecting you?"

"No," Steve answered. "We would like to talk to him about how he started his business. I know a little about the old Cal Neva Casino."

Steve turned toward the picture that contained the image of the casino as he continued talking.

"And I really would like to ask him how he started his business on the site of the old place."

"What is your last name?" the receptionist asked.

"Mitchell, Steve Mitchell."

The receptionist picked up the phone and called Mr. Slater's office.

"Sir, there is a Steve Mitchell here to see you."

"Mr. Mitchell . . . hmmm, I don't recognize that name. What does he want?" Tom asked.

"He would like to talk to you about how you started your business."

"When is my next appointment?"

"Not for another hour, Mr. Slater."

"Okay, I'll be right up," he replied.

Tom walked down the hall to the front desk and introduced himself to Steve and Julie. He was a good-looking man in his midsixties. He was well dressed and had a healthy physique. There was no doubt the man had been successful in life. He carried himself with confidence.

After the introductions, he led Steve and Julie to the glass-enclosed conference room.

"Have a seat. Can I get you anything to drink, water or coffee?" he asked the two of them.

Both declined.

"Well, I understand you are interested in how I started my business. Is this for an article you are doing?" Tom asked.

"No, not an article," Steve chuckled.

"I have a connection in the past to the old Cal Neva Casino, and it appears you have built a really fine establishment right where it once stood. I was curious if you knew the owner. I believe his name was Jake."

Tom leaned back in his chair and interlocked his arms behind him. A smirk came to his face as he answered Steve's question.

"Jake, good ole Jake Malone . . . now there is a name I haven't heard for a number of years. I didn't know him, but I knew of him. Wow, that's a long time ago. I guess indirectly he is responsible for me being in this business."

"How is that?" Julie asked.

She continued to take notes as Tom answered.

"Well, you see ole Jake got himself in trouble with the gaming commission back in the early sixties—late 1962 if I remember right. The rumor has it he was quite connected to the mob. Some bad stuff went down in '62, and it came back on Jake. One thing led to another until the feds stepped in and locked the doors.

"Jake was in a world of hurt after that. Seems all kinds of stories came out of the woodwork, implicating him in a number of crimes. It took a couple of years, but they finally nailed him on racketeering and a few murder charges. The courts didn't take kindly to that because it gave the commission a black eye for not investigating sooner.

"Yes, Jake got slapped pretty hard. They gave him life in prison with no chance of parole. The feds sent him to San Quentin to serve out his sentence. That's the last I heard of him."

"Well, how did that help you get a hold of the property you now have?" Steve asked.

"When Jake went to prison, the feds took control of the Cal Neva for good. It had been shuttered for a couple of years as the courts did their thing. By the time the feds got the property under forfeiture laws, it was pretty well run-down, and they decided to auction what they could and bulldoze the place.

"I was a young guy back then, and I dabbled in real estate somewhat. I was never really successful in it, but I kept trying. I had a feeling the tourist industry would grow in this town, and I thought if I had a bunch of shops that the locals could sell their goods at, the tourists would buy them.

"I heard about the auction of the Cal Neva and decided to bid on a couple of the lots they had. One of the lots contained an old Chevy sedan. It seemed to be in okay shape, but the driver's window had been busted. The seats were pretty well trashed from sitting with that window missing for a couple of years. But I thought that with a little loving that I could get the thing running and resell it for a few bucks.

"I got the thing home, and after a couple of days, I opened the trunk, and there in plain sight was a gleaming brick of gold."

Steve swallowed hard. It was at that moment he realized the car Tom bought at the auction was the same one he drove into the parking lot back in 1962. Steve had managed to steal two of the gold bricks from Billy and Luke at a roadside motel—one he used to frame Billy and Luke and the other he left in the trunk of a Chevy sedan. The car was the same one that the thug busted the driver's window with his fist at the Cal Neva before dragging Steve to Jake's office.

Tom continued. "I sold the gold for a lot of money, and after that, the rest is history. The banks finally loaned me the money for my business plan, which allowed me to secure the property where the Cal Neva once stood. From there, it was off to the races, building what you now see today. Of course, we have made many improvements over the years.

"I called my business Chevy Properties because of that old car. I wish I would have kept it. It would have been a good thing to put behind glass in my lobby."

Julie was dumbfounded with Tom's explanation of how he started his business. She knew Steve's story, and it was just so amazing to her to hear the same story from another person's account.

"So Jake went to prison. Did he die there?" Steve asked.

"I'm not sure," Tom answered. "I never heard any more about him after he went to San Quentin."

Steve had heard enough. He had the lead he was looking for to begin his search for the missing gold. That lead was Jake Malone. Steve stood and reached his hand out to shake Tom's.

"Tom, you have been very helpful. You undoubtedly are a very busy and smart business man. Thank you so much for taking time to share your story. I had a . . . let's call him *distant relative* that knew Jake somewhat, and I might just have to track Jake down in prison and find out when he died or if he did. We are going to be on our way. Thanks again."

Julie shook Tom's hand also as the three of them exited the room. On the way out of the building, Steve made a point to thank the receptionist for her help. As they left the building, Steve was excited that he now had a lead on that day back in 1962 albeit that lead most likely was dead now. At least he had something to go on.

More Clues from the Library

Steve and Julie drove out of the parking lot with questions about what their next move would be. They both knew that the trail was going to start with Jake and what became of him. They had to verify Tom's story before moving forward.

Julie asked Steve, "What should we do now?"

Steve replied, "I suppose the best thing would be a visit to the local library and research some old newspaper articles that could be helpful in giving us insight on what became of Jake. What did Tom say his last name was?"

Julie looked back in her notes.

"Here it is. Malone. His name was Jake Malone."

Steve pulled into a nearby service station and asked the attendant where the local library was. Turns out it was just a few blocks away.

Steve and Julie entered the library and were met by a frail old woman. She quietly introduced herself as Martha. She paused and stared at Steve intently. Finally, she realized she was staring and excused herself.

"Pardon me for my stare, but you look so familiar. Have we ever met?" she asked.

"I don't believe so. I'm not from around here. My name is Steve Mitchell, and this is Julie Stanton. We're here to do some research regarding an old casino that once was here in town."

"Sonny, I've lived here all my life, and I've seen plenty of 'em come and go." Martha chuckled as she spoke.

"What casino are you interested in?" she asked.

Steve answered, "The Cal Neva Casino from the sixties."

"Well, that one I know very well. I worked there as the head teller right up until the feds shut it down. It was my first real job of importance."

"Is that right? How interesting. I guess I've come to the right place. I understand the head of the casino went to prison. I'm curious if you might lead me to some of the news clippings from that time as to the trial of Jake Malone. Is that possible?" Steve asked.

"Sure, it's not only possible but easy too. The Daily News covered it extensively. Being I worked at the casino, I took an interest in most of the news articles that would come out. Kept 'em all right here in this scrapbook."

Martha went behind her librarian counter and pulled from the lower shelf a dusty old bound book with newspaper clippings. She placed it on the counter and slid it to Steve.

"There ya go, sonny. Research away," she said with a smile.

Steve opened the dusty relic, and the first article contained a black-and-white photo of Jake. He cringed as he stared at the photo. This was the same man that was responsible for numerous deaths. He was the same man that tried to kill him but failed. Here it was years later, but to Steve, it was like yesterday. The attempt was still fresh in his mind.

Steve and Julie thumbed through the book until they came to the article describing the sentencing phase of Jake's trial. The article read,

> Today, the Tahoe area court system handed down the strictest of verdicts for Jake Malone's murder and racketeering convictions. As the jury foreman handed over the document to Judge Tyler, Mr. Malone sat restlessly. Judge Tyler looked over the jury's decision before addressing Mr. Malone and his legal team. He then turned to the defense table and asked the defendant to please stand. Mr. Malone and his legal counsel stood but not without apprehension.
>
> Judge Tyler read the charges of racketeering one by one, and after each charge, the judge pronounced "Guilty as charged." The court then sentenced Mr. Malone to 120 years to life, and he was turned over to the proper authorities for immediate transfer to the federal prison in San Quentin, California. Mr. Malone was visibly shaken.

Steve closed the book and thanked Martha for being such a great help. Julie and Steve discussed their next move as they walked back to the car. They both agreed a visit to San Quentin was in order. It was thought that they might find out a little bit more about Jake and who he associated with. So it was settled; they would make the four-hour drive to San Francisco in the morning to visit San Quentin.

Chapter 3

The Next Day

Early the next morning, Steve sat on the hotel patio, nursing a cup of coffee. The view looked out over the lake. It was a gorgeous view to say the least. The air was calm, and he could see a fog bank at water level slowly dissipating in the early morning sun.

Steve was already packed and just waiting for Julie to come down from her room. His thoughts took him back to that eventful flight just a few days prior when he was flying over the very lake he was looking at. He still questioned how he could have been transported back in time. Here he was remembering the entire ordeal as it just happened, but in reality, so many years had passed since the experience. It played on Steve's mind.

"Well, good morning, Mr. Mitchell."

Steve turned to see Julie, ready to travel. Her silhouette against the sunlight made her appearance like that of an angel. He chuckled at the sight because he had experienced the same thought when he visited the 1860s and saw Jean in the same manner. How odd, he thought, how some things never changed regardless of the year.

"And a good morning to you, gorgeous," Steve replied.

They greeted each other with a gentle hug and a kiss. Steve offered to get Julie a cup of coffee, but she said she already had hers in her motel room. Steve finished the last of his and grabbed Julie's luggage.

As they headed to the car, anticipation was high for the day's activities. Neither knew what to expect when they got to San Quentin. It was a long shot at best, but they had to follow the trail of the gold, and there was no doubt that the trail started with Jake.

As they drove out of Lake Tahoe, Steve made a call regarding the Curtis Helldiver plane he had purchased to George Masters.

"George, Steve here."

"Well, hello, Steve, how are you feeling?"

"Not too bad, healing up nicely. Say, how is the repair on the plane coming?"

"Steve, it's going to be awhile. I'm having a real hard time finding that canopy. I've checked a lot of the salvage yards, but no one seems to have one for that model. I've got several I'm still waiting on a callback from, but I'm fairly confident I'll find one. It just may take a bit," George answered.

"That's what I thought may happen. No problem, George. You have my number. Call me when you get it together."

"Will do. You staying in town while we get it done?"

"No, Julie and I have some business down toward San Francisco we need to take care of. Once you get that done, I'll come back and pick up the plane. Do you think the check I left you will be enough to cover your expenses?"

George answered, "Oh sure. If not, I'll call you. Have a good trip to San Fran."

"Will do, George. Thanks."

Steve hung up the phone and turned onto Highway 50. It was a gorgeous morning. The wind blew gently through the leaves on the trees, turning them in different directions, showing the brilliant colors they were made of.

Julie asked, "Steve, what do you think we are going to find when we get to San Quentin?"

"I'm not quite sure," he said.

"At the very least, I'm hoping to get a hold of Jake's prison file. Maybe that will shed some light on the people Jake may have stayed in contact with or visitors that may have come by. I just don't know. He was incarcerated there so long ago. We need to find out what happened to him."

Julie was quiet for a little while. She was in deep thought about Steve and the amazing travels in time he had experienced.

Finally, she said, "Time is a funny thing, isn't it? You somehow managed to see things a long way in the past. I mean—my goodness—the 1860s! That's a long way back. If you told someone what you have experienced, they would think you were crazy."

"Julie, I know. I can't figure it out. Why me? If someone told me they had seen and been where I have been, I would think they were crazy too. One of these days, I hope to have an answer. But for now, all I can do is accept that it was real whether anyone believes me or not."

"Oh, Steve, I believe you. I wish you could know how much I believe you."

The rest of the ride to San Quentin went quickly. Steve and Julie talked about a lot of different things from the weather to politics. But Julie was holding back a little. She had her reasons. The time was not right. She knew when it would be, but Steve had to be in the right frame of mind to accept what she had to say.

San Quentin State Prison, California

Steve and Julie arrived at the prison shortly after 1:00 PM. The place was more massive than they had envisioned. The visitor-parking lot was only about half-full. Steel fencing and razor-barbed wire were in abundance. A sign on a walkway stated, in bold letters, "All visitors must enter here."

They walked toward the guard at the entrance. He was sitting behind a fortified glass wall. The two sleuthing amateurs were intimidated with their surroundings. Neither had been this close to a maximum-security prison before. Steve told Julie he would do the talking.

"Excuse me, sir, but I am a freelance writer for a historical magazine in Saint Paul, Minnesota, and this is my assistant, Julie. We are doing an article on an old casino in the Lake Tahoe area. There once was a prisoner incarcerated here by the name of Jake Malone that was associated with the former Cal Neva Casino. Could you lead me to the administration building so I may inquire as to his records of incarceration here?"

Steve was doing his best impression as a reporter. He was feeling confident he would be given access to the administration, but after that, he was not sure what he would say to gain access.

The guard just chuckled. "You mean ole Jakey boy. No need to look at his file. Why not just ask him?"

Steve looked at Julie, and both were startled.

"You mean he is still alive?"

"Oh yeah, he is a fixture around here. I think he just turned ninety-two, but he still has it all together. Surprising though, he hasn't had a visitor in years. He keeps mostly to himself, reading. For the most part, he behaves himself, but when he gets cranky—good Lord, ain't no one want to be around him.

"Still want administration, or would you like to visit him yourselves?" the guard asked.

"You know, I think we would like to visit him in person."

The guard got on the phone and made the necessary arrangements for a visitation. Steve was stunned that Jake was still alive.

After checking Steve and Julie's identification, the guard instructed them to go to the waiting room at the end of the hall and said someone would let them know when Jake had been transferred to a visitor cell.

While in the waiting room, Julie suggested to Steve that maybe she should go in first and talk with him to prepare him for what he was about to see. Steve agreed; otherwise, the shock may be too great for him. He's gotten older, but the man he knew as Steve in 1962 still looked the same.

Jake's Cell

Jake was reading a book when the guard came to his cell door. Although he was ninety-two years old, he didn't look like it. He was still very coherent, and the exercise through the years kept him from becoming too frail.

"Jake, you got a visitor," the guard grunted.

"A visitor . . . me?"

He closed the book he was reading and walked to the cell door.

"What do you mean a visitor? I haven't had a visitor in years."

"Just what I said—a visitor. In fact, there are two of them: Steve Mitchell and Julie Stanton, and the lady is real fine. You sly ole dog, you been writing to some of those mail-order brides?"

Jake was taken by total surprise. No one had visited him for several years now.

"Well, Jim, you going to stand there and gab, or are you going to let me out to see my visitors?"

The guard smirked as he joked, "Jake, you are the most cantankerous ole codger we got around here."

"Well, if you don't like it, then leave the jail door open," Jake snidely remarked.

The guard just laughed. He called on the radio to open cell door 726. The door electronically opened with a clang. Jake and the guard followed the maze of catwalks and stairways on their way to the visitor cellblocks. Jake was silent during the walk. He had an uneasy feeling about this visit. In the past, he would have some advanced warning when someone would be visiting. This time was different.

Visiting Room

The guard let Jake in the room, and as procedure, he remained at the back by the door until the visit was done. Jake uneasily sat down in the wooden chair and faced the glass that separated him from the visitors. He still had a bit of apprehension about this visit. Visitors had stopped years ago. His thought was *why now*?

Steve explained to the guard that Julie was going to go in first to describe the nature of this visit to Jake. The guard led Julie into the room that faced Jake. It was cold and uninviting.

As she walked toward the thick glass, she could see Jake's disconcerted appearance. The wrinkles that lined his face showed a man that had been void of a meaningful relationship for years. Julie picked up the phone that connected her to Jake and spoke first.

"Hi, Jake, my name is Julie Stanton."

"They told me you were pretty, and they're right . . . but who are you? What do you want with me? Interviews were done years ago," Jake replied.

His demeanor was matter-of-fact without showing emotion. He did not want to show his true apprehension hidden deep within him. He listened as Julie continued.

"This is kind of hard to explain, Jake. But years ago, you were involved with a crate of gold. There was a pilot at that time. His name was Steve. There seems to be a lot of unanswered questions about that time and, quite frankly, questions that have no logical answers."

Julie was expecting some sort of reaction from Jake, but he just sat stone-faced without showing emotion. Julie decided no further explanation was going to change his perspective. She decided to just blurt out her purpose.

"Steve is here to see you. I came in first to hopefully explain a little so there won't be too much of a shock."

Jake continued to sit stone-faced without commenting or reacting to Julie's words. He had an idea on what was about to take place, but he was prepared. He thought about this day for years. Although he didn't show it, he was still very much apprehensive on what was about to take place.

Julie saw he was hesitant to answer. She did not know how to take this. It made her feel uneasy, so she just excused herself and said she would get Steve.

Julie left the window to go get Steve. He rounded the corner, and both men just stared at one another for several seconds. Julie stood behind Steve, watching the reactions of both men. Steve slowly sat down on the bench facing Jake. He picked up the phone while Jake's stone-faced composure turned into a smirk.

"Hello, Jake. I can see you remember me."

"Yes . . . yes, I do," Jake said sarcastically. "I was wondering when you would show up."

"You mean—you expected me?" Steve asked, surprised.

"Yeah, I did. That day in my casino office when Billy had a choke hold on you and then you simply vanished into thin air told me that moment was something of the paranormal. Something also told me it was not the last I would see you.

"A lot of bad stuff went down after that day. Too much water has gone over the dam, and I ended up here with a whole lot of time on my hands. I've done a lot of reading while in here. Seems you might have experienced what I've been reading about. You're proof there is something to this time-warp subject. No one has an explanation on how it occurs other than it does happen occasionally. I've aged. You haven't. So there's my proof to what I've been reading about. But it does me no good. What brings you here to see me?"

Steve sat stunned. Julie had no reaction. Steve finally began to speak.

"Hmmm . . . interesting, I thought you were dead and come to find out you are alive. I then became concerned the shock would be too much on you, and now I find out you were expecting me. Life is just full of surprises these days."

Steve sat back and chuckled out loud. He then moved closer to the window separating him and Jake. Steve stopped his chuckling and spoke with intensity.

"Listen, Jake, I'm not going to beat around the bush. I can see I don't need to, so I'm going to lay it on the line. You see, I know all about the mob gold and how it was meant to pay off the Russians to assassinate President Kennedy. I know you planned to waste me. I followed Billy and Luke to the spot where they buried the gold. You see, I get the big picture. Back then, Samantha filled me in on all that was happening. But what happened to the gold after Billy and Luke stashed it? I know it's not there. I've checked. Were you involved with President Kennedy's death in '63?"

Now it was Jake's turn to chuckle, and chuckle he did before answering Steve's question.

"Once a punk, always a punk. You got some of your story right but not all of it. I'm going to tell you something I have never told anyone or admitted to any of the charges against me. After this, I can die in peace."

Jake had Steve come closer to the window as his speech turned to almost a whisper.

"Yes, the gold was to pay the Russians for a hit on the president. That's what my associates voted to do. But I was never for the plan. I wanted nothing to do with knocking off a president. It's un-American.

"After you were to drop the gold, Samantha and her boys were to sink the Russian ship along with the crew. They then were to run with the gold. I had it worked out so they could hide undetected until the heat blew over. My associates would think the Russians nabbed the gold and never made good on their promise.

"What I didn't plan on was Billy and Luke going off the deep end and planning a heist to take the gold themselves. They paid dearly for that, but I'm not going to get into that."

"But what happened to the gold?" Steve interjected.

"Hold tight, scrappy, I'm getting there. You were so intent on following Billy and Luke out of Trinidad that you never saw the person following you. You're a real good sleuth, aren't ya? You still don't get it, do you?"

Steve's facial expressions gave it away. He was confused as to what Jake was getting at. Jake continued.

"That person following you was Samantha. You don't think she was going to let that gold get away, did you?"

"So Samantha dug up the gold and took it?" Steve asked.

"Yep, sure did. But I didn't expect her to double-cross me. She disappeared that night with the gold. I swore I would find her and make her pay like Billy and Luke did. But I never did, and I ended up here.

"I'm not sure where she's been for the last few decades. Word on the street is my counterparts found out about the plan. Good thing I've been in here, relatively protected from the outside world. There is a hefty price on my head for doing what I did or planned on doing. It never did quite come together as I had counted on. Yep, the price on my head is a hefty one that those on the outside would love to cash in on.

"Recently, I've heard they found Samantha in the Minneapolis area. She's living incognito off Jamaica Avenue in Cottage Grove, Minnesota. She's moved quite a bit since '62. She needed to. You might want to check out a restaurant called the Pasta Palace in downtown Minneapolis."

"What about the gold?" Steve asked

"That I'm not sure about. But if she still has it, I would say she's in a world of hurt now that—ah—*certain people* know where she's at. One thing I am sure of: if that gold falls in the wrong hands, it could buy a lot of grief for someone.

"Well, that's it, Steve. I'm out of the loop, and this interview is over. You're on your own. Good luck on whatever you're trying to accomplish. You're going to need it."

With that, Jake got up, turned from Steve, and walked away. As he left the visitors room, he felt the demons in his soul of so many years had been vindicated. He finally told the truth to someone. Jake went back to his cell and, within days, passed away from a massive heart attack. He went to his grave without telling anyone except Steve the full story of that day back in 1962.

Julie and Steve Sit Perplexed

Steve and Julie watched Jake leave the room. Both felt they had received more information than they bargained for. Jake being alive was shock enough, but to actually hear firsthand what happened to the gold left Steve at a loss for words.

They left the prison and headed to the nearest café in town to think this new information out. They found a roadside establishment complete with blinking neon lights. Julie and Steve walked in and found a quiet table in the corner. The locals looked at them as they had at so many others: as just other visitors to the penitentiary. Steve and Julie sat in silence for a moment, both not knowing what to make of the conversation they had just encountered. Julie broke the silence first.

"Steve, what are we going to do? Should we go to the authorities with this?"

"I don't know, Julie. My head is spinning. That night back in 1962, I thought Samantha was sincere. I thought she wanted out of that life. How could

44

I have been so wrong? I just don't know what the answer is. I never thought Samantha was in on such an elaborate plan to thwart the mob's intentions. I guess it now makes sense why she was so nervous when I landed the plane at the Eureka Airport. That's when we both thought the gold was on board.

"If we go to the authorities with this story, they're liable to lock me up as a mental patient. I suppose our best choice is to go to Minnesota and see what we can find out about Samantha before Jake's counterparts do. When she left me that night, she said that if I ever got to Minnesota to look her up. She said her name was Samantha Thompson. I guess I should take her up on that. If Jake is still alive, maybe she will be too."

Steve and Julie sat in silence for the next few minutes, each nursing a cup of coffee. Steve was contemplating on what to do. He wondered whether he could believe Jake's story. He weighed the options he had. Was the story true, or was Jake just a silly old man was the question he had to answer.

Meanwhile, Julie had her own moments of contemplation. She had some dark secrets, and her story was just beginning to unfold. Steve had no idea of the surprising news she wanted to reveal. She thought about if the timing was right and how she could actually bring the subject up with Steve.

Chapter 4

The Moment of a Shocking Revelation

Julie and Steve had just finished visiting Jake Malone, the Cal Neva Casino owner who was in prison for life. They were sitting in a roadside café, discussing the information Jake had given them. Steve was contemplating his next move while Julie was trying to find the courage to bring up an important matter of her own to Steve.

There was an awkward few minutes of silence as both Julie and Steve reflected on their individual issues. Julie decided to break the silence first while they sat in the café. It was now or never. She no longer could speculate whether Steve would accept the truth.

"Steve, what do you think of what Jake said regarding his reading?"

"You mean about time travel?" Steve asked.

"Yeah, I know you have experienced it, but do you think others have experienced the same thing?"

Steve pondered the question before answering. He never really thought of anyone else experiencing it. He just knew he had, but now that the question had been raised, he mulled over the subject before answering.

"Well, I suppose it's possible. After all, it happened to me, and I am no one special. But I have to say I honestly never really thought of anyone else doing it. I just know it happened to me."

Julie was quiet, not wanting to ask, but her emotions compelled her to continue. She had to ask Steve.

Without blurting it too loud, she questioned, "Why did you leave me on that dance floor?"

Steve had a puzzled look on his face. He had no clue on what she was talking about. They had not been dancing yet.

"Julie, what in the world are you talking about? What dance floor? When did I leave you?"

Steve was a bit indignant with his questions back to her. He had so much to think about with the information Jake gave him, and now Julie was asking about dancing? It was an absurd question to him.

"Like I said, why did you leave me on that dance floor back in the 1860s when Jack cut in on our dance and you left with Jacob and Leroy? Why didn't you come back? You left me, Steve, and I never knew why."

Julie's emotions were strong at this moment. Years of being jilted unexpectedly and without reason bubbled over uncontrollably. She could see Steve's face going flush and the shocked look on his face. He was beginning to realize what she was referring to. First Jake's news, and now this from Julie; it was an almost-unbearable amount of information to comprehend. Both were in a state of disbelief, but Julie remained in control of the conversation.

"Yes, Steve, you are not the only one that can travel into the past. There are others that travel in time too—just not backward. They jump forward. Steve, I'm one of them. I'm Jean!"

The news to Steve came as a total shock. Never did he expect this. He stuttered as he spoke.

"You mean Jean . . . Jean from the 1860s? The one I fell in love with? The schoolteacher? How did you—"

"I don't know," Julie interrupted. "I just know that when you didn't return, I was angry. Jacob, Leroy, and Jack returned, laughing about how you ran like a church mouse and that you were shouting 'I'm never going to return.'

"I took the wagon and horses and rode hard for my place. I was humiliated. I rounded the corner a little too fast and felt the wagon tipping. Next thing I knew, I woke up in a new world. I woke up in a strange new place, not knowing where I was. Come to find out it was an apartment."

Steve listened intently. He left Jean in a world far away in the 1860s and never had a chance to explain his absence. Now that same woman was sitting before him in 2012, untouched by the aging process. When he first saw Julie in the hospital back in Minneapolis, he was shocked to see how much she looked like Jean. But he never associated her as being Jean. It took him by so much surprise that he couldn't talk. Julie continued.

"I know this is a little much right now. But just like you expected me to believe you, I expect you to believe me. We are a different breed. We have been blessed with something that defies all human beliefs. Why, I don't know."

Steve finally mustered the strength to talk.

"How long have you been here?"

Julie talked softly, realizing the enormity of the conversation.

"I've been here quite a few years. When I first awoke in my apartment, I was frightened. I had no idea what had happened. It took me by such surprise. I didn't leave the apartment for a couple of days. It took me that long to convince myself that my life as Jean was nothing more than a vivid dream. I internally examined my life and discovered I somehow knew nursing. I knew where I lived. I knew how to operate a television for goodness' sake! That's why I lived for years thinking the life in the 1860s was merely a dream.

"But then you came into the hospital after your plane crash, and I recognized you as the man I fell in love with back in the 1860s. I couldn't figure that out. I still was not convinced it was nothing more than a dream. Then you revealed to me about your experience of going back in the past, and that is when I knew it was real. I knew I was Jean, and I knew I had to stay with you until the time was right to tell you."

Steve, still stunned by the revelations, finally was able to coherently put his thoughts to words. Although it was difficult to grasp the enormity of the situation, it was beginning to sink in that Julie was Jean.

He looked at Julie with sincerity in his eyes as he said, "I never wanted to leave you on that dance floor. They stuck a gun in my side, and I decided I had to go with those idiots so they wouldn't hurt you. They were trying to kill me. I had every intention of returning.

"Those three idiots made me run for my life and yours. I was trying to get away from them when I dove headlong into the river with my hands tied behind my back while trying to elude their gunfire. Next thing I knew, I was waking up in the hospital. It was a surreal experience.

"Julie—or Jean, I should say—I loved you then, and I love you now. I don't know why we have been chosen to live this life but we have. We are going to have to try to find the good in it."

Julie had tears in her eyes as Steve spoke. She had waited for this time since that very first sight of Steve in the hospital. She had found her love again.

The two of them embraced with a newfound admiration for each other. Steve brushed the tears from her eyes as he said with a smirk, "I guess I'll have to start calling you Julie Jean."

Both smiled and embraced again. Julie had waited for the embrace for some time. Although they had embraced before, this one was different because the wall of secrecy about her past had been torn down. Steve now knew the truth about her background.

"What do we do now?" Julie asked.

"I guess we are off to Minneapolis to look up Samantha Thompson," Steve said.

The two of them made the necessary arrangements to make the flight from California back to Minneapolis. They gathered their things and headed for the airport.

Three Days Earlier—Thailand

It was 3:00 AM when April's cell phone rang. She was sound asleep in her hotel room. Her travels with merchant marines were interesting, and it took her to some exotic places as well as let her meet some very unsavory characters. The life she now lived was a far cry from her life in Hawaii and engagement to Steve years earlier. She never questioned her decision to break off the engagement but did question her choice on the direction her life had taken since then.

It took her a few seconds to realize what the ringing was. She answered it, still half-asleep.

"Hello."

"April, it's Mom."

"Mom? Why are you calling so early?" she asked.

Samantha Thompson, her mother, answered in a whisper. Her voice was in a panic. She was cowering in a bedroom closet with her cell phone pressed tight to her face. Outside the closet door, several men were busy tearing apart Samantha's bedroom. Her husband was tied to a chair, being pistol-whipped. The men were repeatedly asking him questions as to where the goods were.

"I don't have much time, so listen to me closely."

April, now fully awake, sat up straight in bed.

"Mom, what's wrong?" she asked in desperation.

"I said listen to me! If I disappear, you need to get an envelope hidden in the house."

April was shocked and confused by her mother.

"What's going on, Mom?" she blurted.

"April, don't interrupt. Just listen to me! I said I don't have much time. There are things you don't know about me."

April could hear the muffled screams of her father in the background. She began to panic. She listened intently to what her mom was saying.

"In the bedroom, next to my nightstand, the carpet is loose. Pull it back, and there you'll find a floorboard that has been cut away. Pull that board up, and in the space behind it, you'll find a key and an address to a storage unit in town. Go there and clean out the contents. Don't tell anyone! Just take it and disappear."

April was now completely confused.

"Mom, what—"

"Listen, April! I haven't always been the good mother you thought I was, and I'm sorry for that. The truth is the mob is after me for some things I've done in the past. I can't change that, and I don't want you involved with my troubles. There is a small Italian restaurant near Nicollet Mall and Seventh downtown. It's the local hangout for these guys. Stay away from the place. There's a back room that—"

Before she could ask her mom any more about what she was saying, she heard the closet door open. She could make out the sounds of someone throwing her mother around the closet she was hiding in. A man growled obscenities at her as he pulled Samantha from the closet. He growled as he ripped the phone from Samantha's hand.

"Who is this?" the man yelled into the phone.

April remained silent but trembling.

Again the man screamed, "Who is this?"

"What do you want?" April managed to whisper.

The man broke the phone in half and threw it against the wall. April's phone went silent.

"Mom . . . Mom!"

The phone remained silent. April pulled her legs into a fetal position and trembled. She was half a world away, and she just heard her mom being accosted, and there was nothing she could do.

Several years ago, she lived a simple life in Hawaii while waitressing at one of the local seaside restaurants. She had a brief affair with a military man but soon ran from that when he proposed marriage to her. She didn't want to settle down as of yet.

During the same time, a gentleman would visit the restaurant regularly. He was involved heavily with world trade. The man would share his adventures with April and tell her of the exotic places where he had been.

April, like her mother, Samantha, had an appetite for adventure. So when the man suggested that she come travel with him, April took little time in making up her mind.

On one hand, she was being offered a life with an air force pilot who undoubtedly loved her and would cherish her deeply. He would give her a stable life. On the other, she could travel and see the world and not know what the next day would bring. Her appetite for adventure won the battle of her heart versus the stable life she was being offered.

She went to her fiancé's apartment early the next morning and left a note saying she couldn't settle down now and that she was sorry. April left that day with the vagabond world merchant.

Her life that followed was not what she expected. She found herself caught up in a trade market far away from the American life she knew. It was a market that included danger, illegal trades, and numerous characters that were the complete opposite of the stability of the air force pilot she left behind.

April now sat in her Thailand hotel during the early morning hours, thinking of the phone call she just received from her mom. She wondered if the people she was involved with had anything to do with this. She trembled at the thought. She cried softly for her mother.

Minneapolis International Airport

April watched the Minnesota landscape get closer as the airliner made the landing approach. The time she spent awake on her flight from Thailand to Minneapolis was filled with thoughts of her mother. Her associate, Mario, traveled with her.

Mario was the man in Hawaii that convinced April to leave her fiancé and travel the world with him. He was of Brazilian descent. His physique was that of a fit man. His black hair flowed to his shoulders, and his facial features, with its olive skin tone, gave him the look of a well-to-do individual. He was always impeccably dressed.

April knew Mario had some questionable contacts throughout the world. His various secretive meetings and rendezvous would cause her concern, but up until now, she never questioned them. She thought that the less she knew, the better off she would be.

As April watched the Mississippi River go by from the airline window, she thought of her childhood days. She, being the only child, spent hours on the river with her father in his boat. He taught her how to ski. He taught her to ice-skate. He had taught her so many things.

April had no idea what to expect upon her arrival home. She had called the local police from Thailand to report her mother's frantic phone call, but upon inspecting the outside of Samantha's home, the police saw nothing amiss to warrant entering the premises without permission. They told April to contact them if she had any further word.

Now all April could do was to wait, wonder, and speculate. It took forty-five minutes to get through customs. Once they were cleared and their luggage was retrieved, the two headed for the rental-car counter. In thirty minutes, she would be at her mother's home. She had no idea what to expect. Her concerns were for her mother and father. Mario's concerns were for what was hidden in the floorboard of the bedroom.

Thirty Minutes Later—Minneapolis International Airport

Steve and Julie arrived at the Minneapolis Airport shortly after April and Mario had landed. They had a location of 555 Jamaica Avenue in Cottage Grove to visit. Julie had searched the Internet for the last name *Thompson* on that street in Cottage Grove and found one possible address location.

Steve was feeling apprehensive to visit because of the time that had actually passed since 1962. He had met Samantha back then, but this was now some years later. Just as his visit to Jake in San Quentin, Steve looked the same, but she would be older. He wondered what she looked like now and if she would remember him.

Julie and Steve retrieved Julie's car from the parking lot where she had left it days earlier to go visit Steve in Lake Tahoe. Steve climbed in the driver's seat and embarked on the same roads as April and Mario had en route to 555 Jamaica Avenue in Cottage Grove. A showdown was ahead that neither April and Mario nor Steve and Julie had expected.

555 Jamaica Avenue

April pulled in the drive of her parents' home. Just as the police had reported, nothing was amiss on the outside. Her mother and father moved quite frequently. She fumbled in her purse for the house key Samantha had given her on a previous visit a few months earlier.

Walking up the steps to the front door made her fearful to what was behind it. She placed the key in the door and turned the tumblers while Mario nervously looked on. He consistently glanced over his shoulder at the surroundings. He was used to watching over his shoulder. The door opened with a squeak.

"Mom? Dad? Anybody home?" April questioned through the open door.

There was no answer. April and Mario cautiously entered the house, leaving the front door open. Once inside and away from the window's sight line, April's fears began to escalate. The furniture had been overturned, drawers and their contents were strewn about, and broken glass was scattered over the floor.

"Mom, where are you?"

April cautiously climbed the stairs to her parents' bedroom only to be disheartened again. The room was in total disarray. Even more frightening was the evidence of dried blood. April sat on the floor and cried. Her worst fears from the frightful phone call Samantha made to her in Thailand appeared to be true.

Mario knew that the entire ordeal could get out of hand if the police were called. He had things to hide and did not need to be in a police-interrogation room and be asked questions.

"April . . . April, listen to me," Mario said.

Mario knelt down next to her to console her, but his real intention was to get what they came for and leave. He had been intrigued as to what was hidden in the floorboard ever since April relayed Samantha's phone call to him. Such a hiding place suggested it was something of great importance.

He continued. "What happened to your parents is out of our control. We can't reverse whatever has become of them. Listen, sweetheart, we need to get what your mother left in the floorboard and get out of here. Do you understand? We need to leave this place."

Mario's interest in the whole ordeal was piqued. He wanted to know what was so important in the floorboards that April's mom would risk her life for it.

April whimpered a little more and agreed to Mario's reasoning. She went to her mother's bedside and moved the nightstand. Just as Samantha had said, the carpet was loose. She pulled it back, revealing the floorboard. The board had two cuts approximately eight inches apart. Nails had been driven into the floorboards on either side at an angle to keep the cut floorboard suspended in place.

April lifted the cut floorboard from its position. She reached inside and felt around for what was left in there by her mother. She pulled from the opening an unaddressed envelope. She opened it and pulled out a blank piece of paper that had an address printed on it with a key taped to the bottom. The address read, "1230 Robert Street, West Saint Paul, #220."

"Does that mean anything to you?" Mario asked.

"Not a thing," April responded.

Outside 555 Jamaica Avenue

Steve and Julie drove slowly down the street, searching for the house number of 555.

"It should be the next house on the right," Steve said.

He pulled the car to the opposite side of the street across from the tan-colored house. He placed the car in park and scoped out the house, not knowing what he was going to see. In the driveway was a white Chrysler 300, but other than that, nothing seemed out of the ordinary.

"Let's just sit here a minute and observe," he told Julie.

Both watched as they saw the front door of the house open. From the open door stepped out April and Mario. Steve took a double look and couldn't believe he was seeing his former fiancée from when he was stationed in Hawaii.

"Well, I can't believe this," Steve said.

Without explanation, Steve opened his car door and stepped out. He was headed straight for April. He gave no explanation to Julie. His surprise to seeing April took over his actions.

Julie was in a state of astonishment by Steve's actions. He gave her no warning. Julie hurriedly exited the car and chased after him.

"Steve! Steve! Where are you going? What are you doing?"

Steve just kept charging forward without answering Julie's call. He wanted to know why April was here at Samantha's house.

His thoughts were racing. He had met April while stationed in the service where a deep but brief romance ensued. He had asked her to marry him, and she accepted but quickly broke it off unexpectedly with Steve. He never associated her with Samantha, but now he was focused on it. He approached April, who was startled by his presence.

"April, it's Steve."

April was surprised by Steve's approach. She had no idea why he was here at her parents' house. She was unsure what to expect next.

"Steve, it's been a long time," she awkwardly said.

"Yes, it has," he replied. "What brings you here?"

"Here? Maybe I should ask you what brings you here to my parents' home," she retorted.

Julie had now caught up to Steve and was standing by his side. Confusion was written all over her face.

"I'm looking for a lady by the name of Samantha. Is that your mother's name?"

"Yes, it is," April responded.

April was in no way interested in staying to chat. She was in a hurry to leave. She didn't want Steve to know what she knew.

"Listen, Steve, we are in a hurry to meet a deadline. So I can't stay and catch up on old times. I hope life is treating you good."

With that, April turned to open her car door. In her haste, she lost her grip on the piece of paper she had in her hand, and the wind blew it to the ground at Steve's feet. He bent down and picked it up and handed it back to her. But before handing it back, he saw the address printed on it and the key taped to it.

April quickly grabbed the paper from Steve and climbed in the car. Mario hurriedly jumped in the passenger seat. She started the engine and quickly drove down the driveway. Steve remained in the same spot and watched her leave. He was now as confused as Julie.

At the end of the driveway, April stopped the car and opened the driver's window. She called Steve to her car. She had things she wanted to say to him.

"Listen, Steve, I can't just leave without saying something. What we had was good, but it wasn't for me. I feel bad the way I left. I don't want to see you caught up in my affairs. So a word to the wise: don't go in the house. Just walk away."

"April, this is not about you. You left me a long time ago. I think I've recovered from it. This is about your mother. I need to find her."

"My mother? Why would you want to talk to my mother? Oh, never mind. I don't want to get involved with your affairs. I need to go, but a little advice to you, Steve: don't go in the house. Just leave—leave now."

April put the car in drive and quickly left. She and Mario were on their way to the address Samantha had written on the piece of paper that was hidden in the floorboard. Steve and Julie were left standing in the driveway with a lot of questions in their minds.

"I get that was your old girlfriend, but what do we do now?" Julie asked.

Steve sighed as he answered.

"Yes, that was an old girlfriend from my time in Hawaii. But that is not my concern now. My concern is, what was she doing here? I don't know what is behind that front door, but from the way April was talking, it doesn't sound very good. We can't just break in and see for ourselves. We have no reason to be in there. We can't go to the police because whatever is in there would implicate us. We have to do what April said and just walk away.

"But there are two things we have. The first is the address I saw on that paper April dropped. It had a key taped to it. I'm going to assume it's some kind of storage. The second is we have a lead on people that may have known Samantha at that restaurant downtown that Jake gave us. My guess is we go to that address I saw on that piece of paper April had. I think that is going to be our best bet now."

Steve and Julie heeded April's advice and did not enter the house. They returned to the car and headed for the address in West Saint Paul. They figured April was headed directly there also. It was their hope to be able to see what it was April was after. Steve had a good idea that it was the gold.

To get to West Saint Paul from Cottage Grove, the road crossed the main railroad tracks from the south. It was a busy line, and multiple trains daily would stalemate the traffic leaving town. As luck would have it, a multiengine train was just starting a slow trek at the crossing when Steve and Julie approached. Steve's delay gave April and Mario a twenty-minute advantage to get to the West Saint Paul address.

1230 Robert Street, West Saint Paul

April and Mario arrived at the Robert Street address. The sign read Robert Street Storage. They followed the driveway to unit number 220. April had mixed emotions. She did not know what the key she had from her mom would reveal. She had no idea what her mom was into. The thugs she overheard on the phone took her mom from her before she had the chance to discuss it.

As April thought about that final night on the phone with her mother, it made her become increasingly angry. She continually was thinking,

Who were they, and what did they want? She knew that it had something to do with that restaurant downtown. She wanted to do something about it.

The storage unit was smaller than what April had expected. Mario took the key and placed it in the lock and gave it a turn. The lock popped open, releasing the locking mechanism on the overhead door. Mario raised the door, revealing several small crates stacked against the back wall.

April and Mario approached the crates and removed one of the lids. Inside the crates were gold bricks that glistened in the light.

"Gold? My mother was sitting on a stash of gold?" April exclaimed.

"I've got to tell you, I didn't expect this," Mario responded with disbelief.

Both ran their fingers over the gold, petting them like they were kittens. Mario had not expected this. His mind began to calculate his next move.

"You know, April . . . I have a feeling whoever was in your parents' home was after these crates. I suggest we load them into the car and leave quickly. I don't want to meet up with whoever your mother did."

April agreed. Both quickly transferred the gold to the car. They wanted to leave as quickly as possible. They worried that they were being watched.

The train cleared the crossing, allowing Steve and Julie to continue toward the address in West Saint Paul. They arrived at the storage unit just as Mario and April sped around the corner. Steve managed to catch the license plate number of the car: UBC 271.

Before Steve could get turned around, April and Mario had disappeared into the city traffic. Steve quickly told Julie to write the license plate number down before he forgot. Before leaving the storage area, they examined the inside. Mario and April had left hastily. They did not close the overhead door to the unit. Inside, Steve saw nothing that caused suspicions. The only things the storage room contained were a few empty crates strewn about the back of the room. As they were leaving, his eye caught a piece of paper behind the guide rails of the overhead door. It was small and just seemed like a torn scrap of paper. Steve reached down and picked it up. He turned it over, and on the back side was a handwritten phone number: (612) 873-5698. He had no clue if it held any significance to his quest. He shoved the paper in his pocket.

Steve Ponders the Clues

Steve decided to go to his office and try to sort out all that has happened thus far. His office was not far away, and in a few minutes, they would be there. They had some clues but nothing concrete as of yet, but questions did abound.

Steve parked the car in front of the entrance. He knew the comfort of familiar surroundings would help him think more clearly. So far, they had the name of Samantha Thompson, her daughter—April, Jake's confession of the gold, and a scrap of paper with a phone number on it.

Steve made a pot of coffee. He sat at his desk while it brewed. The aroma filled the office. Julie stood by his trophy case, admiring the crude carving of a Cessna 310. It was hard to fathom that it was made by Steve over a hundred years ago. They both were there when he carved it back in the 1860s.

"Steve, you know I think we can get to the bottom of this. Look at this carving. Who would have thought we would ever see this years later? I mean, we are destined for something. Look at what we have been through."

"Yep, we sure have been. But I'm not sure what we're trying to solve as of yet. There must be a purpose somewhere," Steve remarked.

Steve and Julie began discussing what they knew so far. They had knowledge that Samantha had the gold. They deduced that the gold had now fallen into the hands of April and her friend. But the question was for what purpose, or was there a purpose?

Steve searched the Internet for the phone number that was on the piece of paper he found at the storage unit. The number belonged to a restaurant at the corner of Nicollet Mall and Seventh Street in downtown Minneapolis that was called Pasta Palace. This was the same restaurant Jake had told him about.

Researching the restaurant revealed that two years prior, there had been a drive-by shooting at the restaurant. Three people were gunned down while they sipped wine on the patio out front. The perpetrator or perpetrators were never caught.

Steve wondered if there was a connection to the piece of paper and the restaurant. More importantly, did it have anything to do with April and her unsavory friend?

Steve and Julie decided it would be a good idea to visit the restaurant downtown. They left the office and headed for the Pasta Palace. They were unprepared for the reception they were about to receive.

The Pasta Palace

Steve pulled his car to the valet stand at the front of the Pasta Palace Restaurant. A young man in a dark suit quickly greeted them and opened Julie's car door for her. She exited the car with a smile and a nod. Steve handed the keys to the attendant in exchange for a valet ticket. Another classily dressed gentleman opened the front door to the restaurant.

The lobby was adorned with Italian marble and numerous statues. There was no mistake that the place had some money backing it. Steve and Julie quickly realized that it was not your average Saturday-night-date restaurant. This place was for the who's who of the city. Autographed portraits of famous athletes and Hollywood stars plastered the walls.

Steve approached the maître d' to introduce himself and ask for the manager. But before Steve could speak, the maître d' held up his hand to hush Steve.

"I know who you are. Please wait here for a minute." The maître d' hurried down the hallway and disappeared into a side office. There, a man sat behind a bulky desk, smoking a cigar and reading a financial report. His name was Eddie.

Eddie was the main boss here in the United States for the Moretti crime family based in Verona, Italy. The harsh actions of their members reached worldwide. The Morettis ruled with brutality, instilling fear into anyone who associated with them. The family was known to be arms dealers for many third-world countries. The network of high-powered attorneys kept the organization one step ahead of the law.

The maître d' spoke first. "You were right, Eddie. He's pretty smart. How did you know he would find us?"

"Simple," Eddie responded. "He's been trained to follow through. He has to see whatever he is doing all the way to the end. That's why I wanted him to fly the package that day. If he hadn't crashed, there is no doubt in my mind that that package would have made it to San Francisco."

"He's with a lady. Want me to send just him or the both of them?" the maître d' asked.

"Yeah, send them both in," Eddie responded. "Then tell Larry and Bud to be ready."

Steve and Julie stood in the lobby, waiting. Julie was feeling very eerie about being in this place. She reached out and squeezed Steve's hand. She pulled him closer and whispered in his ear.

"Steve, I have a bad feeling about this place."

He whispered back, "Don't worry, sweetie. I won't get us into anything I can't handle. You're safe with me."

The maître d' left the office and went back to the lobby area. He motioned to Steve and Julie. "Follow me. I'll take you to see Eddie," he told them both.

Steve was unsure of who the maître d' was taking them to go see.

He whispered to Julie, "Stay close to me."

Julie once again took Steve's hand. Her palms felt sweaty in his hand. Steve knew she was very uncomfortable by being in this place.

The maître d' led Steve and Julie into Eddie's office. Eddie sat staring at Steve and Julie. He took a puff from a half-used cigar and placed it in the ashtray. Steve extended his arm to shake Eddie's hand. Eddie shunned his advance and leaned back. The chair groaned under the weight of the big man.

"Sit down," Eddie growled.

His face looked menacing as though he had a beef to take up with them. Steve and Julie did as the man commanded and sat at the two chairs in front of the big man's desk. Eddie continued with a matter-of-fact attitude. He was a man of no compassion. In his opinion, there was God, his father, and then Eddie. All others were beneath him.

"No need for formalities. You know who you are, and I know who you are. One thing I don't know, and I'm going to assume you do, is what you did with my shipment."

Steve had no idea as to what Eddie was referring to. Steve could not recall ever meeting him or having any business with him. Steve leaned forward in his chair as he spoke.

"Sir, I'm a bit confused. Shipment? What shipment?"

Eddie gave a sinister chuckle as he rose from his chair. He walked around to the front of his desk and sat on the edge.

"Well, let me refresh your memory. It seems to me that several weeks ago, I sent a courier to your office with a crate and $75,000. You were to take that to San Francisco and deliver it. Next day, I read in the paper of a plane crash and that the pilot is in a coma at the hospital. We had no contract—didn't want one. So to recover my property through the authorities was useless. But as you may have guessed by now, I have ways around authorities. My boys discovered the crate was missing from the crash site.

"We paid you a lot of money to move that. My guess is with that kind of juice riding on a simple little crate, you realized you had something of value, and without a contract—poof, my shipment and my money are gone."

Steve indignantly replied, "Mr. Eddie, or whoever you are, you are totally wrong on your accusations. That crate was on my plane safe, secure, and unopened when I crashed. I resent being accused of something I did not do."

Eddie rose from his seat on the edge of his desk and towered over Steve. The tone he answered in was low and quite threatening.

"You can resent all you want, and I could care less what you think. All I want is to get my property back."

Eddie returned back to his chair. He pressed a button on his desk, and two of his henchmen, Larry and Bud, entered the room.

As he sat back in his desk chair, he said, "Okay, here's what's gonna happen. The way I see it, you let something of value get out of your hands. I don't know how or care to know why, but one thing is for certain, you will find it and return it intact."

Larry and Bud moved closer to where Steve and Julie were sitting. With one quick move, they picked Julie up out of her chair and started carrying her to the door. Julie was in a state of panic and shock.

"Steve! Steve! Do something!"

Steve immediately rose from his chair only to be pushed back by one of the men.

"Don't be a dead hero, cowboy," Larry said.

Steve, still wanting to come to the defense of Julie, instinctively tried to stand again only to be pushed back by the man once more. Steve continued to fight back only to be subdued each time.

Eddie yelled, "Get her out of here!"

The two men left with Julie kicking and screaming. Steve grabbed the sides of the chair and tensed up. His breathing was heavy as he watched Julie disappear out the door. He turned to Eddie and started to address the man.

"If you think you're gonna get—"

Eddie cut Steve off before he could finish his sentence. His tone of voice was even more ominous.

"Shut your mouth! I'm calling the shots here. You have one and only one choice: trade my crate for your girl. Period! I don't care how you do it, but if she means anything to you, you will find a way. Now I suggest you get off your hero instincts and go find my crate."

Steve stood, placed both hands on Eddie's desk, and leaned over the desk as he indignantly answered.

"Let me tell you something. I didn't take your blasted shipment, but I will find it, and when I return with it, if I find one hair out of place on her head," Steve leaned further over the desk with both hands resting on it, "I will make sure you pay with your life!"

Eddie retorted, "Get out of here before I make you both pay with your lives!"

Steve turned and stomped out the room, slamming the door as he left. His heart was pounding. All he could think of was Julie and her safety. He kept hearing Julie's voice in his ear, saying she had a bad feeling about being at this place. Also going through his mind were Steve's reassurance to her that he would protect her.

He got to his car, which the valet already had waiting. There was no need for the valet ticket. Steve hurriedly sped away as he was thinking of what he was going to do next.

The Back Room

Julie was led down the narrow hallway to a sparsely lit room. Against the back wall was a run-down, dirty couch flanked by a wooden chair on either side. The single lightbulb hung from a wire in the center of the room, casting its glow on the interior that was dreary and uninviting.

The two men pushed Julie through the door and made her sit on the musty couch. It made her skin crawl to come in contact with the soiled cloth. Both men took a seat on the wooden chairs at either end of the couch.

No words were spoken. The larger of the two men stared menacingly at Julie. After a short time, Bud stood and said he was going to grab a bite to eat. He left instructions with Larry to stay alert and keep to himself. The only response was a grunt and a smirk while all the time he never broke from his stare of Julie.

As the man walked from the room, he pulled the door shut, startling Julie. She did not want to be left alone with this man. She did not trust him.

"So, pretty lady, ever desire a bad man like me?" Larry asked in a sinister tone.

Julie tried to ignore his comments and just looked away. She was frightened by the man's look. She did not want to encourage a confrontation.

The man rose to his feet. His movements were slow and deliberate as he loosened the belt he was wearing.

Julie, trying to defuse the situation, said, "I don't think your partner will be very long. I'm sure he is just around the corner."

The man continued his slow advance toward Julie. He pulled the belt from his pants. He wrapped the ends of his belt around each hand and pulled tight. The grin he displayed became more evil by the second.

Suddenly, the man leaped forward and grabbed Julie. She tried to scream, but the big man had placed the belt across her mouth like a horse bridle. Julie was petrified.

"If you struggle, it's just going to make it worse, pretty lady. We're gonna have a little fun, and you're going to like it. Do you understand?" Larry sternly said.

Julie just stared at him with fearful eyes. He pulled the belt slowly from her mouth. Julie was shaking with fear. She thought of how much she would want to see Steve come busting through the door. She knew the chances of that happening were slim.

Julie decided she was not going to make it easy on this creep. As soon as the belt was removed, she began to scream and thrashed about. She hoped that there would be someone on the other side of the door to rescue her. But it was not happening.

The more she fought, the more the man pinned her down. He had one hand wrapped firmly around her neck while the other tore at her blouse. He squeezed harder and harder on her windpipe. She felt as though she no longer was in her body but rather was above the scene, watching it all play out. She felt her spirit move further from the scene until darkness surrounded her.

Larry's massive hand fell flat on the floorboard. He could not believe his eyes. Julie just vanished into thin air. He slumped to the floor, trying to determine what just happened.

A short time later, Bud returned with a few burgers and fries. He saw Larry slumped in the corner, looking dazed and confused.

"Larry. Larry. Hey, Larry!"

This startled the big man back to reality. But he was at a loss for words.

"I don't know, Bud. I just don't know. She vanished right before my eyes."

Bud gave a swift backhand to the side of Larry's face. He scolded him for his incompetence.

"You idiot! I leave you with a simple job of just watching the girl, and you can't even do that. I'll bet you tried to . . . ah, you useless piece of flesh."

Bud threw the bag of food to the wall. His anger was almost uncontrollable. He knew he had to have an explanation and soon, or Eddie would have them both killed.

"Did she go out the door or what? How did you let her get away?"

Larry became increasingly aggravated with Bud's accusations. He lashed out at Bud.

"Listen, dimwit, do you think I would let her go on purpose? I can't explain it. One minute she's lying on the floor, and next minute, she's gone. Poof—vanished—disappeared! I don't know how or why, but you better quit giving me so much grief, or we're both going to be in a world of hurt. Now let's figure out what we can do to rectify this problem before Eddie finds out."

Both men let level heads prevail and started working on a plan. It was decided that Larry would go tell Eddie that Julie was giving them too much trouble and that they were going to take her to the lake house. There she could scream and kick all she wants because no one was going to be around to hear it.

Eddie bought the plan and told them to head up there and not to speak to anyone unless it was him. Larry and Bud cleaned house and vanished. They escaped by the thinnest of margins.

Steve's Dilemma

As Steve drove away from the Pasta Palace, his mind was deep in thought. He was anguishing over the fact that he allowed Julie to be taken from him. What took place at the restaurant was furthest from his mind when they walked into the place. He replayed the scene over and over in his mind, trying to determine what he could have done differently.

He questioned himself about contacting the authorities. It was a perplexing proposition. If he did, would it somehow get back to Eddie's gang and possibly put Julie in even more danger?

Steve had no real knowledge of just how powerful Eddie's organization was. But it wasn't hard to figure out. He decided to leave the authorities out of it for now. No telling what city official was on his payroll.

He thought about the crate he was carrying when he crashed. He knew now that it was Eddie that hired him to fly the crate to San Francisco. Although he saw it contained a lot of gold when he was transported back to 1962, it still didn't add up. He realized now that Samantha took the gold from the hideout back then. From what he saw in the crate back in 1962, he assumed the gold ended up on his Cessna 310 when he crashed for the first time just a few months earlier. But did it? He thought, *Maybe Samantha had the gold all the time and the gold wasn't in the crate that fateful day I crashed? If it wasn't, what was?*

Steve had a lot of questions to answer quickly if he was to save Julie. He had to start somewhere. Maybe the answer could be found with April. His new quest had begun in earnest, and in his mind, the answers needed to come quickly.

Chapter 5

Mario's New Plan

After Mario and April safely exited the storage unit with the gold on board, Mario made a quick calculation of their stash. He figured it was worth a multimillion-dollar cache! This now created in his mind a mountain of possibilities.

Before reaching the airport, he had April pull into a local park. He told her he needed to make a call. April stopped the car, and Mario stepped outside to make his call. He paced back and forth excitedly as April watched. She couldn't hear what he was saying, but she knew he was concocting a plan.

"Asad, it's me, Mario. Let me talk to Aziz. It's urgent."

Aziz came to the phone.

"Yes, Mario, what is it?"

"Aziz, it's amazing! You'll never guess what has happened."

"Please, Mario, no games. Just tell me. Are the triggers safe?"

"Yes, the triggers are safe. As you know, our helicopter that was following the plane when it crashed found them before the authorities arrived. They flew them directly to our command center, and they are still there. The Morrettis have no clue that we have them."

"Good, Mario, you keep a watchful eye on that. We need those triggers to complete our plan."

"That's just it, Aziz, our plan! I went with April to her mom's house, and some bad stuff went down there. Not sure what, but it was bad. Her mother, Samantha, left April a pleasant little surprise. It was in her storage unit. It was gold bars, Aziz!

"I figure we have millions of dollars in gold. It got me thinking. You know how we planned on hitting the financial markets to create havoc in the American system? Well, I thought, wouldn't it be better to take their money at the same time?"

Mario had Aziz's interest intensified. "Yes, go on," he said.

"Let's use this trigger device we have to bring down a financial powerhouse in an area away from Wall Street. Investors would be threatened by a financial-market hit. They would shy away from the paper investments and automatically look to a safe haven—gold. This would double, triple, or who knows maybe even quadruple the price of gold today. This would make our new windfall stash of gold worth even more than what it is today. We collapse their system and at the same time line our pockets with their wealth."

"Mario, that's an interesting twist. We need a face-to-face meeting. I think you may have something here. Have you told April?"

"No, but she does know about the gold."

Aziz replied, "Hmmm, that may be a problem. Meet me at the command center tomorrow."

"What about April?" Mario asked.

"Keep her close until I arrive. She needs to be watched. She is not to go anywhere alone. Do you understand? Nowhere."

Mario acknowledged the command.

Aziz's Militia Group

Aziz was the leader of a small militia group that wanted to make a name for itself against a powerful nation, namely the United States. He grew up in southern Alabama as a son of a preacher man. His American heritage waned in his high school years. Being a poor preacher's kid left a stigma on him that he couldn't shake.

In his early twenties, he tired of the American establishment and turned to a Far Eastern religion and took on the name of Aziz Mohammed. He renounced all forms of his upbringing. His parents were devastated and lost all contact with him.

Aziz formed a tight-knit group of misfits that were focused on taking down the financial markets. Numerous times they schemed and collaborated with each other on ways to bring calamity to the financial markets on a national scale. They would rest on nothing less than success.

While on a cruise to Mexico, Aziz met Mario, and the two became the best of friends almost immediately. The bond of friendship was cemented with each other's distaste for organized governments.

Aziz soon found out that Mario, being a merchant marine for some time, had created numerous contacts with arms dealers around the world. This piqued Aziz's interests even more. One such dealer Mario was associated with was the Morretti family.

Mario managed to collect the components of some very dangerous and powerful dirty bombs. The only things lacking were the trigger mechanisms. He was in the process of dealing with some previous sellers in obtaining the triggers when a special British task force spooked the seller's organization. They ended up going underground before Mario could complete the transaction.

It wasn't until Mario made contact with the Morretti family in Italy that he found a new source for the triggers. He was told to contact a man in a pasta restaurant in downtown Minneapolis if he wanted to make the deal.

Mario followed through and met with a man named Eddie at the restaurant. Shortly thereafter, a deal was cut to buy the triggers needed to activate the dirty bombs. Mario's money man, only known as RD, was in San Francisco. He was spending a lot of money to get these and wanted to see them for himself before handing over a lot of cash.

The Morrettis hired Steve to fly the triggers to San Francisco under the guise of "artifacts." RD had his concerns on there being a government sting operation, so he had a Jet Ranger helicopter with Aziz's men aboard follow Steve's Cessna 310 on his way to the West Coast that fateful day in late spring.

When the plane went down, Aziz couldn't let the triggers be found. He had his men have the helicopter pilot land, and they grabbed the triggers from the wreckage. He now had what he needed to make the bombs complete, and best of all, he didn't have to pay the Morrettis for them. He thought they would think they were destroyed in the crash.

Aziz knew it was important to keep it under close wraps that they had the triggers. He knew the ruthlessness of the Morrettis, and he was counting on the power of the Morrettis for future arms procurement.

Steve's Office

Steve, back at his office, sat silently at his desk. His mind went over and over the events of the day. He tried to determine where his starting point was. He couldn't help but think of Julie. *Is she okay? Is she hurt? Does she know I am going to fix the situation?* These were the thoughts that clouded his consciousness, making it difficult to concentrate.

The phone rang, startling Steve back to coherency.

"Steve, it's Frank at the tower."

"Yeah, Frank, what can I do for you?"

"Well, I don't think you can do anything for me, but I think I can do something for you. I got the records on your crash back from the NTSB. Seems I was mistaken on that helicopter following you on your crash day. It wasn't registered in California after all. It was registered to a company in Minneapolis called the Portillo Fund LLC located at the corner of Nicollet Mall and Seventh. They keep it up at the Anoka Airport."

"Do you have the N-number?" Steve asked.

"Yeah, it's N2455."

"Hey thanks, Frank. I gotta run. Thanks again."

Steve had his starting point. It was with that helicopter. He hurried out the office and was on his way to the Anoka Airport. He wanted to investigate the lead on this helicopter as quickly as possible.

Waiting It Out

Mario finished his phone call with Aziz and went back to the car. Aziz and Mario were concocting a plan to use the gold they had in the trunk of April's rental car. Mario knew he had to take control of the situation from here on out with April. He went to the driver's door and opened it.

"April, sweetie, let me drive."

April undid her seat belt and slid from the driver's seat and stood next to the driver's door and questioned Mario.

"So what's going on here?"

Mario, not wanting to create any more tension in her than what she already was displaying, asked her politely to get in the car.

"Not until you tell me what's going on."

Mario told her again, "April, this is not the time or place. Now get in the car."

April could tell by his tone of voice that he was aggravated. She stormed around the front of the car to the passenger side and got in with an attitude. Her emotions, already in shambles over the last several hours, were brought to the edge.

She continued badgering Mario from the passenger seat as he put the car in drive.

"I'm confused, Mario! I mean, what is going on? I'm already a wreck over my mom, and now you're being so secretive. Tell me right now. What is going on?"

Mario stayed silent and just drove away. April can see she wasn't getting anywhere and turned to look out the window. A tear slid down her cheek. She had so many questions—questions about her parents and questions about the gold in the storage unit.

As Mario pulled the car away, he turned north. He was going in the opposite direction of the airport. He had heard April's questions but couldn't answer them. There was so much going through his mind. A lot was riding on the gold he had with him from Samantha's storage unit. He liked April, but he now considered her expendable. He could see she was going to be in his way.

A couple of miles before the Anoka Airport, Mario turned off the main road onto a dirt drive. It led back behind a grove of trees to a house that was in need of a good coat of paint.

April couldn't keep quiet any longer.

"What are you doing?" she blurted out.

Mario finally opened up. He wanted to tell her enough to calm her nerves but not to completely tell her everything. He just wanted to keep her calm until he got her in the command center.

"I know you're confused, but you have to trust me on this. I have some very powerful people I am involved with. It's an organization that takes a lot of cash to run. It just so happens we ran into some serious money today, and my people want to make a deal. Go with the flow on this one for me."

"You ran into some money!" April exclaimed. "In case you're forgetting, there is no *we* in this. That came from my parents, and I don't think my mother had you in mind when she told me about it. You just happened to be with me."

April sat stunned, not knowing what more to say. Too much emotion had taken place today for her to try to make any sense out of it all. She decided for now just to stay quiet and see what his next move was going to be.

Mario stopped the car deep in the trees and out of sight of any inquiring eyes. He forcibly led April from the car to the front of the run-down house. He pushed on a wallboard next to the door. A small section swung open to reveal an electronic keypad. Mario entered a sequence of numbers, and the door unlocked.

He pushed April through the door. Once inside, April began to realize she was in trouble. The house was filled with electronic surveillance equipment. Numerous maps were displayed on the walls. There were people sitting in a darkened room, monitoring computer-display screens. The house was a fortress on the inside, and the dilapidated exterior was merely a front.

Mario led April to a room on the far side of the structure. He pushed her inside and closed the door. She could hear the door lock behind her. April beat on the inside of the door with her fist, yelling and pleading with Mario to explain what he was doing. It was to no avail. She could hear his footsteps diminish down the hallway.

April looked around the room. The only thing in the room was a chair and a window on the far side of the room. She went to the window and was surprised to see it would still open. As the window slid to the top, her hopes of escape were dashed. Steel bars covered the outside of the structure.

April went to a lone chair in the corner of the dimly lit room and curled up in a ball, whimpering. She had never seen this side of Mario. She knew he had some rough edges but never imagined the people he was now associated with. He hid his true motivations well. All the things they had done together were now questionable at best. Nothing like what she had seen in the last couple of hours made sense. She undoubtedly lost her parents, and now she feared for her own life. April's life had drastically gone downhill from the moment she touched that gold.

Mario's Organization

Mario returned to the room with the monitors. He went to the corner and looked over the shoulder of a person watching one of the screens. The image displayed the terminal building at the Anoka Airport.

Mario told the operator, "When you see Aziz, you let me know right away."

The operator acknowledged the command and continued watching the screen for any sight of their leader, Aziz. Mario went to pour himself a cup of coffee and to think things out. Life for Mario was changing, and he owed it all to the gold he had in the trunk of April's car.

A few minutes later, the operator spoke up.

"Hey, boss, we got a visitor, but it ain't Aziz."

Mario hurried back to the operator. He too saw the figure the camera was focused on in the lobby.

"Well I'll be, that Steve Mitchell just doesn't quit!"

Chapter 6

The Helicopter Discovery

Steve headed north toward the Anoka Airport. As he drove, he watched the various aircraft on their final approaches to the Saint Paul Downtown Airport. It made him think of the days he first started flying. As a new pilot, he was nervous to enter the landing pattern during the beginning days of his flight training. He wanted to be perfect in all he did on those very first few landings. The same perfection now carried over in his life. He had to do it right. He had to find Julie and get her away from the thugs that held her.

Steve arrived at the Anoka Airport and parked his car at the side of the building. He walked inside the sparsely populated terminal. He was not aware

Mario's organization was monitoring his movements within the building. Steve went to the pilots' lounge and saw an old buddy he nicknamed Chopper. Chopper was busy eating a pastrami sandwich at a counter normally reserved for pilots to do their flight plans.

"Well, Steve, how are ya? Glad to see you're up and moving around these days."

"Hi, Chopper, thanks. It took a bit, but you know me. No one or thing is going to keep me down."

Both men chuckled.

"So what brings you to the Anoka Airport?"

"I'm looking for a helicopter with the N-number 2455. Have you seen it?" Steve asked.

Chopper took another bite of his sandwich and finished chewing before answering. He knew what Steve was getting at. He really didn't want him to go there. Chopper swallowed, then turned to look at Steve.

"Steve, we've been friends a long time, and you know I'm always going to watch your back. So I'm going to tell you something for your own good. Yeah, I know the helicopter. In fact, it's over in hangar 33A. But, Steve, do not go investigating. The people that own that bird are some very unsavory characters. I had a run in with them over airport conduct back a few months ago, and to be truthful, they scare me. I'm just waiting for the day they leave."

"What do you mean they scare you?" Steve asked.

"Can't put my finger on it. I just know something isn't right."

Steve didn't like the sound of things. He had known Chopper a long time, and he wasn't one to back away from mischief.

"Okay, Chopper, thanks. I'll keep a keen eye. You said that was hangar 33A?"

"Yep, Steve, over on the south end, but listen, I don't think it's a good idea to go snooping around over there."

Steve replied to Chopper's warning. "Thanks, I'll call on you if I need anything. I've got to go check this hangar out for myself."

Chopper shrugged his shoulders and simply said, "Suit yourself."

He went back to the pastrami sandwich he was working on. Chopper had determined he was not going to get involved with Steve's affairs.

Steve left the building and passed through security to get to hangar 33A. He wanted to see this helicopter. If this, in fact, was the same helicopter that was flying around his Cessna 310 crash site, it may contain a few clues.

Mario's Watchful Eye

The security surveillance Mario's crew had stationed near the hangar area watched Steve as he entered the tarmac. One of them called Mario on his cell phone.

"Mario, it's Jimmy. It looks like the pilot guy is here and headed for the hangar."

Mario sighed at the news. "I figured it wouldn't take him long to start tracing things back."

Mario turned to the pilot on watch and asked, "You did change the aircraft-logbooks on that bird to show it was parked here at Anoka when Steve crashed, didn't you?"

"Well, boss, I kind of did. You know the FAA was going to have records of that flight, so I couldn't just say it didn't happen. So what I did was I changed it to a mechanical-check ride instead. Hope that's cool with you."

Mario stormed at the man. "No, it's not cool with me! When I give you a job, you find a way to get it done. I don't care what you have to do. Just do it. I did not want that bird showing a flight period."

Mario instinctively reached out and slapped the man. The pilot just took it and didn't say a thing or fight back. He knew what Mario and the organization were capable of.

Mario returned to the monitor. He was becoming increasingly concerned with Steve snooping around hangar 33A.

"Tell Benny to bring up the camera in the hangar," Mario instructed Jimmy over the phone.

Jimmy hung up the phone and knocked on the passenger door of a cargo van parked nearby. It was black with tinted windows and with no markings on the outside. The window opened slightly, and Jimmy relayed the message to Benny inside. He was the individual in charge of communications for the area. The van was a mobile command center able to patch into the various surveillance cameras stationed throughout the area. The Aziz organization had far-reaching abilities for surveillance. Secrecy was of utmost importance if they were to make their stand against the American system.

Benny did as Mario had instructed and patched the cameras stationed near the hangar into a website that only Mario could monitor. Mario sat glued to the monitor, wondering what Steve's next move was going to be.

The Hangar

Steve parked at the side of the building closest to the door. The structure cast a shadow on that side, and he wanted to stay as incognito as possible. Before exiting his car, he surveyed the surroundings. He had remembered Chopper's remarks about the owners of this hangar. Steve was going to make sure he wasn't going to run into the owners while he snooped around.

The area seemed clear of anyone. Steve went to the door, but it was locked. He went around to the aircraft-hangar door, and that was locked too. Steve continued around the building until he got to the back of the hangar. There he found an exhaust duct designed to remove carbon dioxide from the inside. This was going to be his only way of entry if he wanted to leave the door locks intact.

Steve returned to his vehicle and retrieved a tool kit. He went back to the exhaust vent and removed the four screws that held the cover plate on. Once he had done that, he removed the fan motor and laid it aside. The opening yielded a space large enough for Steve to crawl through. He slithered through the opening to gain access to the inside.

Mario saw Steve emerge from the back of the hangar. He watched closely on what Steve was going to do next. He was getting nervous that the cloak of secrecy had been broken. It was now a matter of damage control.

Once inside, Steve saw the sleek Jet Ranger helicopter in the middle of the hangar. The N-number read N2455. This was the helicopter Frank said disappeared from radar for about ten minutes at the crash site of his Cessna 310.

Steve walked around the aircraft, wondering what clues he could gleam from the bird. He climbed inside and looked around the cabin. Nothing gave any clues other than the aircraft logbook. The address showing ownership was a surprise to Steve. It read "R&D Productions, PO Box 2381, San Francisco, CA 94102-2381." This was the same name of the company that was given to Steve when the crate first showed up at his office prior to his Cessna 310 crash.

The logbook also showed a mechanical-check ride the day Steve crashed but nothing about landing or taking off at the crash site. He thought this was odd. He knew Frank from the control tower was smart. He wouldn't make a mistake on aircraft identification. Besides, the transponder showed it descending and taking off from the crash site. Something was not right, but at least now he had a better lead on a location for R&D Productions.

Steve was about to replace the logbook in the pocket it belonged to when he noticed a piece of paper at the bottom. He pulled it out and unfolded the wrinkled piece of paper. It was a receipt for five pizzas delivered about three weeks earlier. There was no address for the delivery, but it did have the pizza establishment's name and address. Plus, it had a transaction number. He stuffed the receipt in his shirt pocket and returned the logbook back to its original location.

Steve left the cabin area and examined the outside of the helicopter. He felt the engine compartment to see if it was still warm. He wanted to see if it had made any recent flights that day. It was cold to the touch. He wandered around the other parts of the hangar. Other than a bathroom, a few storage compartments for fluids, and a tool bench, nothing seemed out of the ordinary. All Steve had was a suspicious aircraft entry in the logbook and the pizza receipt.

Steve left the hangar the same way he entered. Upon exiting, he replaced the fan motor and the covering. He didn't want anyone to notice someone had broken in. Steve was still unaware that he was being watched by Mario and his men the entire time.

Steve left with two clues to work on: find R&D Productions and track down who the pizzas were delivered to. Hopefully, they would yield further clues to finding Julie.

Meanwhile, Julie's New Discovery

Julie was aware of her breathing first. She could almost hear her heart beating. Sounds of a busy street overflowing with commotion filtered through to her senses. She opened her eyes to focus on the scene. Crouched behind a huge slab of broken concrete and standing on its side, she saw the street sign of Nicollet Mall and Seventh Street lying in front of her. The pole had been bent in half, and the signs were touching the ground. It was the corner of the famous FDC Center, the epicenter of the Minneapolis financial district.

Julie was ever so confused. She became aware of the sounds of wailing sirens and people's screams. As she surveyed her surroundings further beyond the broken concrete and the bent street sign, what she saw struck horror to her soul.

The beautiful blue glass that once encased the mighty FDC Center building was nothing more than a heap of twisted steel beams, concrete chunks, and broken walls. The rubble pile spewed smoke from every opening. Miscellaneous office papers fluttered through the air to the ground. Desks, filing cabinets, and every piece of office furniture imaginable dangled from the jagged edges of what was left of the once-fifty-one-story iconic building. Bodies of the dead and dying were strewn throughout the area. Rescue workers scurried, trying to save as many as possible.

It was a scene of horrific carnage. Emergency-vehicle sirens wailed from every direction. Julie tried to gather her thoughts and grasp the enormity of what she was seeing. She had trouble comprehending what she was seeing. Never before had she seen such destruction.

A man in a tattered suit stood by motionless, clutching a briefcase. Julie stumbled over the debris toward the man in an effort to speak to him. The man stared blankly. His clothing was covered in gray soot. He appeared totally stunned.

"Excuse me, sir," Julie managed to say.

The man stood without response. Julie tried again.

"Sir, can you tell me what happened? Can you tell me where I am?"

Again, the man said nothing. Julie was about to lash out at him for ignoring her when a woman wearing a paramedic jacket approached the man. What took place next confused Julie even more.

The woman asked the man what his name was, and without hesitation, he answered her. They held a one-on-one conversation without any lapse in the conversation as the paramedic diagnosed the man for any serious injuries.

Julie, despite being dazed and confused, wanted to offer her medical assistance in any way she could. She thought her nursing skills could help. She reached out to touch the woman on the shoulder only to be totally surprised at what took place next. Her hand went through the woman as though she wasn't even there. Again she tried with the same result. She tried touching the man's shoulder, and once again her hand swiftly passed through him as if he wasn't there.

Julie tried and tried to touch the man and the woman, but each time, her hand went straight through them unencumbered. She heard a man yelling behind her.

"Over here! I've got people trapped, hurry!"

The paramedic turned to the man standing next to Julie. She barked orders at him.

"You're fine. Now go find as many medical personnel as you can. We don't have much time."

The man quickly turned, threw his briefcase to the ground, and headed for a group of bystanders milling about several hundred yards away. The man or the woman never acknowledged Julie standing in front of the two of them. It was at that moment when the shocking realization hit her. She was in a new dimension once again. This time, her leap to the future found herself all alone. The world did not recognize her. She questioned whether she was dead or alive.

Julie moved to a crowd of people she saw standing across the street. The group was huddled around a single individual who seemed to be in charge. The men were conversing on what had happened. From their conversations and the badges they wore, Julie concluded they were with homeland security. She listened as they discussed the distinct probability that a powerful bomb had leveled the building.

Julie listened intently as the men speculated on a new terrorist attack to hit the United States. She wondered if this was for real. Questions in her mind were numerous as to what she was doing there. No one could hear her. She couldn't touch anyone. Communication with the world she was seeing was nonexistent. She was witnessing a terrible scene of destruction. Not being able to communicate frightened her and made whatever world she was in almost unbearable.

Julie turned to go back to the paramedic she first saw, but something strange was happening. As she walked toward the woman, the vision of her faded from Julie's sight. The view of this strange world she was in quickly was becoming dark. The voices faded as the images went out of focus, and once again she was plunged into darkness. She was not seeing. She was not thinking. There was no comprehension. There was nothing but silence.

Steve Traces the Clues

Steve returned to his office to continue doing more research and study the clues he had found inside the helicopter at the Anoka Airport. He sat at his desk and pulled from his shirt pocket the receipt for pizzas he had taken from the helicopter. He held it in his hand and contemplated on how he would get the address to where the pizzas were delivered. He wondered if it even would yield any information that could be useful.

An Internet search revealed no information for R&D Productions. There wasn't any public record of such a company in California. Steve remembered Frank's comment about the helicopter not being registered in California, but instead it was registered to a Minneapolis company called the Portillo Fund LLC.

Steve did a search for the Portillo Fund LLC in Minnesota and, much to his surprise, found the registered address was the same as the Pasta Palace Restaurant where Julie had been taken. He knew now he was on to something.

On a whim, he did the same search in California for the Portillo Fund LLC, and once again he was surprised. The address that came up was "PO Box 2381, San Francisco, CA 94102-2381." This was the same PO box that R&D Productions held.

With these new discoveries, Steve realized now that this was becoming a much-bigger web of deceit than what he first thought. He questioned his judgment on not contacting the authorities from the start. He was rationalizing his thoughts about getting help to unravel the mess. Each time, he came up with the same answer: it was too late. He had to go with the plan Eddie had set before him. Eddie was the one that had the upper hand by holding Julie hostage.

Steve pulled the pizza receipt from his pocket and conducted an Internet search for a phone number to the pizza-business name listed on the receipt. He dialed the number and waited for someone to answer.

"Pizzeria, may I help you?" the voice said on the other end of the phone.

Steve, wanting to get as much information about the delivery as possible, was calm and collected in his response. He politely asked for the manager. The manager came to the phone, and after the congenial introductions, Steve stated his purpose for calling. He began. "Sir, recently a charge showed on my credit card that I don't recognize. It came from your location for a pizza delivery. The transaction number is B3646885. It could have been my office staff, but I'm not sure. Can you be so kind to give me the address it was delivered to?"

"Sure, hold on a minute," the manager responded. "Yes, here it is—500 Fourth Street, Anoka."

Steve, not wanting to make himself sound suspicious, laughingly passed it off as if it was his charge for a customer-appreciation gift. Steve thanked the manager and hung up the phone.

He pulled up the aerial view of the address for the pizza delivery on his computer. The view showed a lone house on the end of a dead dirt road. On the back side of the property was a parcel of land that was densely wooded and with a parallel county road several hundred yards from the house. The house itself looked abandoned.

Steve pondered as to what this property contained. Although the house looked uninhabitable, five pizzas delivered to it said the house contained a lot more people than what the outside showed. Steve decided the house warranted a visit. He studied the computer images of the property, intently memorizing each area as he plotted his next move. He wanted to make sure he knew what was on all sides of this place. He was determined not to be surprised this time as he was at the Pasta Palace. This place would be approached with caution.

The House on Fourth Street

It was 9:00 PM when Steve parked his car on the parallel road next to the densely wooded area that faced the rear of the house. Steve was on his reconnaissance mission. Walking to the front door of the house was not a wise choice. Steve had no idea what or who he would find inside. He wanted the element of surprise on his side if there was going to be one.

Steve sat motionless in the dark before exiting his car. He watched for traffic on the county road. It seemed to be nonexistent. Still he wanted to make sure he was completely alone. In his mind, he was mentally going over the plan he had made earlier in the day while studying the property's aerial view.

After it appeared the area was clear of any prying eyes, Steve slithered out the passenger window, not wanting to open any door that could produce sound or light. He made his trek through the woods effortlessly and in near silence. His military training created an advantage for him.

The end of the tree line was within a few feet of the rear of the house. Steve stopped short of it. He looked over to the rear of the house and the window he faced. A dim light could be seen glowing inside. Next to the window was a darkened corner of the house as if it was jutted out to accommodate a fireplace. On each of the two corners of the house, he could make out surveillance cameras.

At this point, Steve knew he had made the right choice on approaching the house from the rear and quietly. Surveillance cameras on an apparently abandoned house told Steve that whatever was going on inside was not meant for prying eyes.

The cameras made a sweep every forty-five seconds and intersected paths so the entire back of the house was covered by someone watching. If Steve wanted to peer in the window, he would only have a short time span to do so. Steve looked at the fireplace corner, and it appeared that that area might be out of reach of the camera lenses. If he could make it to that corner, it should provide enough cover to not be picked up by the cameras.

He waited several more minutes before making his move. He had to make sure the surveillance cameras were programmed to move and not being operated manually. Being seen was not an option for him.

Steve's heart pounded as he saw the cameras sweep in opposite directions. Decisively, he sprang into action, quickly covering the ten feet of clearing to the window. Before peering in, he ducked into the corner next to the window and froze. Steve could hear the whirring sound of the cameras as they moved back in his direction. He plastered himself to the shadows of the corner.

It appeared Steve was out of reach of the cameras by hiding in the corner. They made the forty-five-second sweep right on time. Steve allowed the cameras to make a couple of sweeps before he approached the window.

Steve saw the cameras swing away from him, and he made his move for the window. As he crouched below the window ledge, he listened intently to any noises coming from the room. He could see the window open but covered with steel bars. The room cast a faint glow of light from inside. He could hear what seemed to be that of a woman's whimper.

Slowly Steve moved his line of sight above the ledge and observed a woman crouched in a chair. He could see the door to the room was closed and no other person was present. It was then that he recognized the woman in the chair. It was April! Steve had not expected this in the least.

"April . . . April, it's Steve," he whispered.

April was startled by the person murmuring her name outside the window. She was a bit dazed and confused as to who could be calling her. She rose and went to the door and listened if there was anyone outside of it. She heard nothing and quickly hurried to the window.

She peered through the bars to see Steve standing outside.

"Steve! I am so glad to see you. I'm locked in this room and in trouble here. I need help."

Steve asked, "What is this place? I need to know what I'm up against. Hold on a minute—surveillance cameras. I've got to move."

He could hear them sweeping back in his direction. He ducked back into the darkened corner. In a hushed tone, he yelled back to April.

"Okay, April. What am I up against?"

April nervously glanced back at the door as she answered.

"Unknown to me, my supposed friend, Mario, is associated with what looks to be some sort of terrorist group. This place is filled with all sorts of electronics. It all went down not long after I saw you at my mom's place."

"April, I know more than you think. I need to get you out of here and take back what you got from the storage unit."

"What?" April sheepishly asked.

Steve replied, "Yes, I'm talking about the gold. It didn't belong to your mom. It belongs to a rough group of unscrupulous people."

April was surprised to hear Steve speak of the gold. She couldn't really understand how he knew. Not knowing how to answer, she denied the knowledge of any gold.

"I have no idea what you're talking about. I just—"

Steve cut her off in midsentence.

"April, cut the crap! This is not the time to deny things. We're both in a world of hurt here. Now I need to know where the gold is so I can save you and my girlfriend."

April's desire to get out of the situation she was in was stronger than her desire to hide her knowledge of the gold. Her demeanor changed to one defeated.

"It's in my rental car."

Steve asked, "Do you have the keys?"

"Mario drove it here," she answered. "Wait a minute."

April remembered they had given her a second set of keys at the rental counter because the car's automatic-door opener was missing from the last rental. The counter attendant was concerned for her getting locked out of the car. April quickly dug in her purse and found the keys.

"I got them!" she excitedly replied.

"Great, now I need to get you out of there. Is there anyone outside your door?"

April hurried to the room's door and listened intently. She returned and told Steve, "I don't hear anyone."

Steve waited for the cameras to sweep away from him again. He worked his way back to the window. He looked at the bars. Fortunately, they were installed directly into the wood with lag screws. Clearly, it was designed to keep someone in rather than someone out. As the wood aged, it loosened the grip of the screws holding the bars in place. Steve looked for what appeared to be the weakest point of securement. After a couple of intermittent trots back to the corner to hide from the cameras, Steve was ready to make his move.

"April, I think I can get a few of the bars off the window. When I do, I want you to climb out as quickly as you can and follow me. Got it?"

April replied quickly with a yes. Steve waited for the cameras to make another sweep away from him. Once they had, he dashed to the window and grabbed two of the bars he had identified as being weakest and gave them a hard yank. They moved slightly. Once again he gave them an even harder pull, and with this one, they gave way, yielding an opening large enough for April to crawl through. Before the cameras could pick the two of them up, Steve helped April out the window. Without hesitation and as soon as her feet were on the ground, he grabbed her hand and ran for the woods. Steve could hear the cameras making their turn toward the two of them.

"Faster!" he said to April.

Just as they entered the woods, the camera swung around to where they had just entered. The branches had not stopped moving. The operator in the command center saw the branches swaying. He stopped the camera on the area to get a better look.

Steve could make out the whirring of the camera come to a stop. He quickly told April, "Drop, now!"

Both of them remained motionless on the forest floor, not making a sound. The camera operator zoomed closer but could not see anything out of the ordinary. He did not see Steve and April. He determined what he saw was just an animal. He restarted the camera sweep once again.

Steve and April resumed their dash for Steve's car at the other end of the forest woods. There was no time to talk as of yet.

The Back-County Road

Pete's car slowed on the county road as he passed a car parked on the side. Something didn't feel right to have a car in that area, much less to be unoccupied. This was not a road that was traveled much.

The radio operator's headphones sprung to life. "Control, this is Pete out on the county road, and I need to run a registration on plate number DJA 0726."

The operator pulled up the website and punched in the information. He responded to Pete.

"The car is registered to a Steve Mitchell out of Saint Paul."

"Really? Better let me talk to Mario," Pete answered.

The operator called Mario to his station and handed him the mic.

"Yeah, Pete, Mario here."

"Mario, I'm out here on the county road at the back of the property, and a car belonging to Steve Mitchell is parked on the side. It appears to be directly across from command. What should I do?"

"Stand by, Pete," Mario replied.

He turned to his crew.

"Listen up, people. Steve Mitchell might be in the area. We just found his car parked on the county road out back. Has anyone seen anything unusual outside or around command?"

Everyone reported nothing out of the ordinary. The one operator that had stopped his camera on the moving branches decided not to say anything. He didn't feel what he saw had any importance.

"Well, keep keen on those monitors. I think he's out there somewhere."

Mario pondered the situation before answering Pete. He decided he couldn't take the chance. Steve must be out there somewhere, and if he is, he may have seen too much. Mario returned to the radio.

"Pete, plant a football under the car."

"10-4, boss. Will do."

Pete moved his car to the rear of Steve's. He retrieved a powerful explosive device nicknamed the football from the trunk of his vehicle. Swiftly he had it attached to the underside of the driver's compartment on Steve's car. He set the timer to explode thirty seconds after the car is started. Once the job was completed, Pete moved his car a half mile away and waited to make sure the explosion was successful.

April and Steve Converse

Steve got to the end of the tree line where his car was parked. He stopped and turned to April to talk. April was shivering from the night air and the fright of the escape.

"April, what in the world have you gotten yourself wrapped up in?"

April whimpered before answering. Steve moved closer and put his arm around her to offer her comfort. He could see she was in turmoil.

"Steve, to tell you the truth, I don't know. My so-called boyfriend, Mario, turned on me. I've seen some rough stuff since my days in Hawaii but never anything like this."

She wiped her nose with her sleeve and continued.

"That house didn't look like much, and when he stopped outside of it, I was confused. I thought maybe he was going to kill me. When we got inside, I knew I was in way over my head. That place is filled with all kinds of electronic surveillance equipment. Monitors were everywhere."

Steve asked, "How many people were in there?"

"I don't know, Steve. Maybe ten, fifteen. I just don't know. Mario quickly ushered me off to that room and locked me in. I was so scared. Still am!"

Steve took over the conversation.

"Listen, I knew your mother. Don't ask me how. There isn't time to get into that, but she was in trouble with the mob."

"The mob!" April interrupted.

"As I said, I can't get into that right now. You know and I know that what you and Mario pulled from that storage room was a pile of gold. Don't get mixed up with it. The people that own it will stop at nothing to get it back. I'm going to help you get out of this, but for right now, I need to get the gold. Is it still in your rental car?"

April looked defeated. She had lost her parents, lost her boyfriend, and nearly lost her life, so she knew Steve was right.

"Yeah, it's in the rental car you saw as far as I know. I'm not sure if Mario has taken it out by now or not."

"Okay, here is what is going to happen. You're going to take my car back to my office. Hit the home button on the GPS, and it will take you right to my front door. I'm going to get your rental car and meet you there. By then I'll have worked out a plan to get you to a safe place. You're going to need to lay low for a while."

Steve handed April his car keys. She rummaged in her purse for her spare rental-car keys. Steve would need her keys if he himself was going to escape from the area.

Before parting ways, April turned to Steve and said, "You're a good man, Steve."

Tears welled up in her eyes as she continued. "You risked your life for me, and for that, I will be forever thankful. I know you didn't have to, but you did anyway. I now wish things had ended differently between you and me. I've come to realize who the man is that I walked away from so many years ago."

She hugged Steve, kissed him tenderly on the cheek, and then turned and moved swiftly to his car. April slid into the car from the passenger window as Steve had directed. She started the car and did as instructed by hitting the home button on the GPS. The map came alive that was to lead April from the sinister grasp of Mario and his gang to a safe haven with Steve. She gave a final look at Steve and smiled, then drove off.

Steve watched April drive away. He had confidence that she would be okay. Now his attention was turned back toward the house. He had to find a way to retrieve April's rental car without attracting attention.

Suddenly, the woods around Steve were illuminated by a huge fireball. He turned to see his car exploding in a massive fireball of melting steel, rubber, and plastic.

Steve dropped to his knees and sobbed. "April . . . no . . ."

Steve was overwhelmed at the loss. He was so sure no one had followed or had seen him. He questioned who he was dealing with and how they got to him. His heart was broken. He sobbed silently but deeply. His once fiancée was gone again. Only this time, she was gone for good.

It wasn't long before his heartbrokenness turned to anger. He was not going to let these thugs get away with it. Steve was determined that Mario and whoever his band of misfits were would not get their hands on that gold. Not only that, but April's death would be vindicated.

His first act of retaliation was to take back the gold. He knew he had the element of surprise, and he was going to use it. The only way he was going to get that gold was to rush the car regardless of surveillance cameras.

The Command Center

Pete smiled as he saw the fireball rise from Steve's car. He called in on the radio.

"Control, let Mario know the football has scored the touchdown."

The radio operator relayed the message to Mario. He smiled knowing he had eliminated an obstruction to the cause.

"Great, Aziz will be proud of all of us," he said to the crew.

Mario went back to making his plans for Aziz's arrival. He had twenty-three bricks of gold to work with. He felt invincible.

The command center suddenly came alive with the sound of lights and buzzers. One of the monitor operators shouted, "Intruder! We have an intruder on the premises!"

The monitors were trained on an individual running from the back of the house to the front. All eyes stared at the screens, including Mario.

"It's Steve Mitchell," Mario shouted. "Quickly, get the guns. Stop him."

The room became extremely active with the mad scramble of people running back and forth. The door was heavily fortified, delaying their exit to the outside. The gunmen furiously worked at the locks.

Meanwhile, Steve's adrenaline was peaking as he ran at full speed to the front of the house. He had no idea what would meet him when he got to the front. He knew he had been seen. Floodlights illuminated the yard as if it was daylight, and warning buzzers sounded everywhere.

Steve rounded the corner of the front of the house and saw April's rental car. Fortunately, it was close to where Steve was. Swiftly Steve was in the car and had it started. He dropped the gearshift to drive and floored the accelerator. Out of the corner of his eye, he could see the front door open and the bluesteel barrel of an assault rifle appear from behind the door.

"This is it. Now or never," he said to himself as he barreled the car through the front lawn and onto the dirt road. He could hear the concussions of the rifles as Mario's men fired at him. A bullet took out the back window and went through the front seat and lodged in the dash. Another shattered the driver's mirror from the door.

In a matter of a few frightening seconds, Steve had cleared the gunfire and at high speed was putting distance between himself and Mario's men. He had the gold, but it came at a very high price. April had paid with her life.

The workers in the command center returned to their individual stations. Mario was furious. He lashed out at everyone, telling them how incompetent they were for allowing this to happen. A low tone of voices could be heard talking back and forth about what just took place.

Mario returned to the desk where he had been sitting prior to Steve's intrusion. He rested his elbows on the counter and placed his head in his hands, replaying the scene in his mind. He was trying to understand why Steve was here. He questioned how he knew which car had the gold. He thought for sure they had blown Steve up in his car.

Suddenly, it occurred to him.

"April . . . no . . . April," he groaned.

As Mario stood, the chair he was sitting on slammed to the floor. He raced off down the hallway toward the room he had April locked in. He quickly unlocked the door and saw the window open. He ran to the window only to see the bars, which once protected her from escape, lying on the ground. It was then he realized who was driving Steve's car. He slumped to the floor, knowing the car he had his people blow up was driven by April.

As Mario faced his demons, Steve drove the car and the gold back to his hangar. From there, he would decide where to stash it until he could determine a plan to get Julie back safely from Eddie.

Chapter 7

Julie's Nightmare Continues

Julie could just barely make out the lights and sounds of a city life. The fog in her mind was lifting. She had just witnessed an unbelievable sight of destruction. Some sort of powerful explosion had ripped the FDC Center building, an icon of the Minneapolis skyline, into shreds. Her presence was not acknowledged by anyone. She could not communicate with a single person. It was as if she didn't exist in that world.

The lights were now becoming brighter. Sounds of taxi horns filled the street. She looked at the street sign she was next to, and it read to be the corner of Nicollet Mall and Seventh Street. But it was no longer bent to the ground as she had seen before. The street sign now stood upright.

Nighttime darkness had enveloped the city. She looked at the building across the street. There stood the FDC Center in all its glory, unblemished in any way. She could see sporadic lights illuminating the various floors. There were no people around. The bank clock showed it was 10:55 PM. Julie reached out to the mailbox on the street corner. No sense of touch existed. Her hand passed through the object unencumbered just as it did earlier during the destructive scene.

A tunnel of light led from Julie to the front door of the FDC Center. She followed it across the street and to the door. The revolving doors were locked, but the side door opened for her without any effort on her part. It was as if it had been expecting her.

Julie walked into the massive lobby. There was no sound except for the rumble of an occasional janitor's cleaning cart. A guard sat directly in front of her. He had a series of security screens that he monitored, but the guard seemed more interested in the portable television he had tuned to the football game.

As Julie walked by the guard, he stood up and looked right at her. She froze and asked, "Can you see me?"

The guard did not answer. Instead, he rounded the end of his station and walked directly to Julie. Her emotions raced. She thought, *Is it now possible to communicate in this dimension I'm experiencing?*

The guard continued on his path directly toward Julie.

She yelled out to him, "Stop!"

He was now a few feet from her, walking at the same pace. Julie's mind raced with all kinds of questions about this crazy time warp she seemed to be trapped in.

He wasn't stopping, and in an instant, he walked right through Julie. He continued on to the water fountain and got a drink of water. Julie now knew she was still trapped in some strange, unforgiving world. She couldn't talk to or feel anyone. It frightened her immensely.

The tunnel of light appeared again, and this time it led to the elevator. Julie continued following it. As soon as she arrived at the elevator, the door opened. She stepped in, not knowing what to expect. She tried but could not push any buttons. Her hand would go right through the walls.

She stood at the back of the elevator, looking at her surroundings, when the door closed. The button labeled *BB1* lit up, and the elevator started a descent to the lowest level of the building. It stopped and the doors opened to a subbasement of the building, revealing a massive pattern of pipes, wires, and low-slung lights.

She stepped from the elevator to follow the tunnel of light once more. She made several turns around machinery and furnaces that kept the building operating.

Finally, Julie got to a long, dark corridor. At the end of the corridor was a work light fastened above a strange-looking conglomerate of canisters and wires. It didn't match its surroundings and seemed oddly out of place.

A lone figure could be seen hovering over this contraption. He seemed to be mumbling to himself. Hesitantly, Julie moved closer to the person. As she walked down the corridor, she could hear another voice that seemed to be giving instructions regarding the machinery to the gentleman.

She yelled out, "Hello? Hello? Can you hear me?"

The person never flinched. Julie got within a few feet of the person. He was reaching over the top and had his back to her. A black bag of tools were at his feet. She had no idea why she was led to this scene.

The man finished reaching around the back of the largest canister and turned around to get a bigger screwdriver. Julie got a good look at him. It was Steve!

"Steve . . . Steve, can you hear me?" she pleaded.

To no avail, Steve was not acknowledging her presence. She had never seen Steve look the way he did. Worry was written all over his face. His eyes had dark circles under them as if he hadn't slept in days. *What has happened to him?* she wondered.

Steve turned back to his work. The conversation that Julie was hearing was Steve talking to someone on his cell phone of which he had on speakerphone. The conversation continued.

"Okay, Mario, now let me make sure I get this right."

Steve wiped the sweat from his brow with his shirt sleeve. Julie could see he was obviously under duress. His blue eyes showed worry and fear. Steve continued the conversation.

"So you want me to pull the cover plate off the back of the large canister, and inside I will find a smaller box with three wires running to it, right?" The phone crackled. "Yes, Steve. The main plate covers a box inside that contains the trigger. Once you have the plate removed, slowly remove the mounting screw and pull the box straight out. Do not let the contacts of the wires to the trigger come in any contact with the metal sides, or the bomb will detonate."

Steve wiped the sweat again and leaned over the canister with his tools in hand. He was doing what the man on the phone had instructed.

Julie could not believe what she was seeing. She wondered if Steve was somehow involved with the death scene she had just witnessed. Her thoughts were *Maybe this was the start of the explosion, and if so, what about Steve? Surely he could not be involved with the sinister actions of a bombing.*

"Okay, Mario. I've removed the trigger box, and I see three wires coming out of it: a red, blue, and a green. Now what?"

Mario responded, "Carefully turn the trigger over, and remove the back-cover plate. Once you've done that, you will see those same three wires run from a terminal inside to a smaller box that will be humming. Be sure to cut the red wire between the terminal and the box."

"So the red wire, correct?" Steve confirmed.

"Yes, any other wire will bypass the timer and explode the bomb."

Steve acknowledged the command from Mario.
Julie started yelling at Steve. She desperately
wanted him to hear her. It was of no use; she could
not communicate in any way. She felt absolutely
helpless.

Steve retrieved a pair of wire cutters from his tool
bag. He then went back to work on the trigger box
as described by the man on the phone. Carefully he
turned it upside down and removed four small screws
holding the back of the box. He let the plastic back
fall to the floor while he steadily held the trigger
motionless so no wire terminals touched any metal.
He could feel the tiny metal box humming inside the
trigger housing. The red, blue, and green wires were
lined up from the terminal junctions to the humming
box just as Mario had said. Steve located the red
wire. It was only about one inch long. His hands
trembled as he opened the jaws of the wire cutters
and surrounded them on the red wire. He paused
momentarily before squeezing the handles of the wire
cutters.

There was no time to hear the snap of the wire.
Julie's world was now operating in slow motion as a
fireball erupted under Steve. She could see his body
being ripped apart and vaporized from the massive
destruction of the bomb. In a flash, he was totally
gone—disintegrated from life. She could not hear or
feel the force as it pulled beams from their moorings.
Shards of glass, metal, and wood dropped from all
sides around her. She could hear nothing nor feel
anything.

Julie felt her body being lifted above the debris that piled up in the subbasement. Her heart raged with anger and fear. She could not believe that Steve would have a hand in this destruction. She continued to be transported from inside the building to the outside. She witnessed the building collapsing downward. Steel and glass littered the Minneapolis streets. The people working in the building at the time became entangled in the mess. The scene was horrific, and death was everywhere. Cars passing the building were flattened by the force of the explosion. No one had a chance.

Julie's awareness was now going dark again. She could feel herself being whisked from the area. The last thing she saw was a man standing with a briefcase and covered in ashen soot. It was the same man she had seen before. She wondered whether it was reality or if she was seeing the events of a diabolical plot before they unfolded.

Steve Stashes the Gold

Steve arrived back at his hangar at the Saint Paul Airport. He knew he had to act quickly to stash the gold before Mario and his band of misfits came looking for him. Steve opened the door to the hangar where he normally stored the Cessna 310. The plane was now gone, so he had plenty of room to maneuver the car inside for cover. After parking, he opened the car trunk to make sure the gold was in place. Once all was secured, he went to his office to figure out his next move.

Steve thought long and hard on what to do. He determined he had to bring someone in from the outside—someone he could explicitly trust. If things go terribly wrong at some juncture, he had to have someone he could depend on to let the truth be known and clear his name.

Hands down there was only one person he could trust with his life. In the service, he had a buddy named Terry Koenig. Steve nicknamed him the Koala Bear. They flew a lot of missions together. After the service, Steve chose to stay in flying while Terry went into law enforcement. He did well for himself and soon became an undercover detective for the Minneapolis police department.

Terry lived in a private community just north of town that shared a grass airstrip with several of his neighbors. He was a hobbyist flyer. Steve decided he needed to contact Terry. He knew he could stash the gold at his place until he could figure out how to get it to the Morrettis in exchange for Julie. Steve placed a call to his buddy.

"Hey, Koala Bear, what are you up to?"

"Steve, I was wondering when you were going to call. It's been awhile."

Steve didn't have time for chitchat. He worried that Mario was not far behind, and he needed to get the gold to a safe place. He continued his conversation with Terry.

"Listen, I need to meet. I've got something I need to keep hidden in your hangar."

Terry asked with confusion in his voice, "Hidden? What's this all about?"

"I'll explain when I get there. I'm leaving right now, and I'll meet you at your hangar."

"Okay, Steve. See you soon."

Terry hung up the phone and was worried about Steve. He could hear the concern in Steve's voice. He knew something was bothering him that was much bigger than what Steve let on.

It was dark when Steve drove the rental car and the gold into the driveway of Terry's hangar. Terry had the door open and waiting for him. Once inside, he closed the door and greeted Steve.

"Okay, Steve, you're here. What in the world is going on?"

Steve never answered. He just walked to the back of the car and opened the trunk. The gold shimmered in the glow of the hangar light.

"Good Lord, what do we have here?" Terry inquisitively asked.

Steve nervously looked over his shoulder and just closed the trunk lid. He told Terry, "Let's go to your office."

Once inside, Steve relayed the story to Terry the best he could without mentioning his jump back in time. He explained how the crate he was originally hired to ferry somehow got him messed up in a shipment of mob gold. Now the Morretti clan is holding his girl hostage for the contents of the crate that turned up missing after the crash of his Cessna 310. He asked Terry to let him stash the gold at his place until he figured out what was going on.

Terry was apprehensive. Being he worked undercover for the police department, he knew just how ruthless the Morretti organization was. He tried to convince Steve to let his department take over. They were much-better equipped to handle this type of situation. He told Steve he was no match for the Morrettis.

Steve knew Terry was right, but he just couldn't chance it. He had to continue the course he was on. He did promise Terry when it was all said and done that he would fill him in on all the players in hopes of bringing down the clan. But for now, he just needed a place to store the gold.

Terry reluctantly agreed, and the two men unloaded the gold from the car into a storage locker in Terry's hangar. Steve knew the gold would be safe.

He thanked Terry and left with the rental car. On the way back to his office, he dropped the car at the rental-car terminal. The place was closed, so he dropped the keys in the night-deposit box and walked away.

Aziz and Mario Meet

Early the next morning, Aziz arrived at the Anoka Airport. Mario was there to greet him. The two of them drove the short distance to the command-center house. Once there, they continued their talk behind closed doors.

Mario reluctantly informed Aziz that Steve had stolen the gold. Aziz was questioning Mario about how it happened.

"Somehow Steve knew about the gold?" Aziz asked Mario in a condescending tone of voice.

"Yes, I think April told him," Mario answered.

Aziz had no time for incompetence. He continued questioning Mario with a raised eyebrow. "And April is no more?"

Mario turned to face the wall before answering. He was gathering his thoughts. He had been with April a number of years but never confided in her his real actions. Now those actions have cost April her life. Mario turned to face Aziz once more as he spoke.

"Aziz, you know how I felt about April. We had a lot of good times together. I feel awful that I never could confide in her my affiliation with our group. I know I couldn't, but at the same time, I also couldn't protect her from the consequences of my actions. I understand you always felt she was in the way. So now, she's not, and let's leave it at that."

Aziz did not care about how Mario felt. Nothing mattered but his fight against the establishment.

Aziz huffed, "That's your battle, not mine. For now, I want to get that gold back from Steve, and I don't care if you have to pry it from his dead fingers. Just get it done."

Mario knew how serious Aziz was and agreed that he would get the gold back. Aziz patted him on the back as if to give his blessing of confidence to him.

Mario knew though that the blessing would only be there if he was successful in his mission.

Mario lingered in the room after Aziz had left. He began thinking on how to eliminate Steve and at the same time regain possession of the gold. He had a devious mind that was working hard at this one. He would find a way to make things happen. He always did.

Chapter 8

Mario Thinks Things Through

Mario, still upset about losing the gold to Steve, decided he had to get really creative to get it back without revealing to the Morrettis that he actually had the dirty-bomb triggers they were going to sell him in the first place. He poured himself a cup of coffee and moved to one of the back rooms in the command center. He closed the door and worked out his plan. He needed solitude to think.

He thought through the events up until now while alone in the room. He first thought of what was the start of the entire ordeal. That was Steve flying the crate that contained the dirty-bomb triggers owned by the Morretti crime organization to Mario's financers in California. When the plane went down,

Mario's crew snatched the triggers from the wreckage before the Morrettis realized what had happened.

Without having to pay for them, it was going to allow the Aziz terrorist group he was associated with to rain terror on the financial markets. Before they could start their plans, his girlfriend, April, turned up with a bunch of gold from her mother. Mario confiscated the gold, and then Steve appeared and grabbed it back. He couldn't understand why April's mom had the gold. Obviously, by the viciousness of the attack against April's mom, this told Mario it was not your average neighborhood gang. He also wondered how Steve knew about the gold.

There was a knock on the door to Mario's room from one of the monitor operators.

"What is it?" he asked.

"Phone call on the private line from Eddie," the operator answered.

Mario looked at the phone, trying to decide if he wanted to answer it or not. His choice was clear: he had to. Mario picked up the phone.

"Eddie, so nice to hear from you."

"Cut the small talk, weasel," Eddie grunted and then continued.

"Word on the street is you wasted April Thompson. I understand she was your squeeze. Too bad, must have hurt. But I don't care. What I do care is that I found out her mother's name was Samantha. Did you know that?"

Mario was trying to figure out where Eddie was going with this conversation. He answered hesitantly.

"Well, uh, yeah."

Eddie continued. "Well, her mother was a distant associate of ours. Seems back several years ago, she disappeared with a stash of our gold reserves. We have been looking for her for some time. Whenever we were able to get close enough to make a move, she would disappear. We recently found her again, and this time . . . well, let's just say we found her.

"Now being April was her next of kin, so to speak, she would stand to inherit what her mother left behind. Do you get my drift?"

"Yes, but what does this have to do with me?" Mario asked.

"Are you stupid or what? The gold, idiot! Did April's mom give anything to her?"

Mario was getting a clearer picture. He now understood that the gold belonged to the mob and they wanted it. This put an entirely different light on everything. This could work to his advantage. Mario knew Steve had the gold, and it belonged to a really bad group of people. Mario did not want to put his cards on the table yet and played dumb with his answer.

"Sorry, Eddie, if I knew she had gold, don't you think I would have protected her a little more?"

Eddie sarcastically answered, "Yeah, I bet you would."

Mario was feeling confident. He decided to bring up another subject to discuss. He wanted to talk about the dirty-bomb triggers.

"Eddie, while I have you on the phone, my finance people out west are getting a little bit skittish about

Rick Oates

not having those triggers. When do you think we can lay our hands on them?"

Eddie did not like the question. He snapped back at Mario with his answer.

"Listen, you tell your people not to worry. I don't do well with pressure from my customers, and I'll pull the plug if they don't back off. You understand?

"Now that we both understand each other, I've located your triggers and will have them to you in the not-so-distant future. Seems our pilot friend tried to play dumb and not know what he took from us, but he has reluctantly put up a little unexpected collateral. I think her name is Julie. But unlike you, Mario, I think he really cares about his girl. I have no doubt he will get the triggers to us if he wants to see her in the shape he left her."

Mario was now totally focused. He surmised Steve had no idea there were triggers in that crate when he crashed his Cessna 310. He must have thought Eddie was after the gold.

Mario abruptly ended his conversation with Eddie. He took a sip of his coffee as he made new plans. He now was going to work on a new strategy—one that would bring him the gold and put Steve on the receiving end of a wrathful mob boss.

Julie Continues to Go Backward

Julie left the man clutching his tattered briefcase on the street corner. She had just witnessed Steve's death and the tremendous destruction of the FDC

Center in downtown Minneapolis. Her world that had gone dark was once again coming to light. She transcended into a room filled with monitors, maps, and electronic gears. This was a place far from the destruction she had seen in downtown Minneapolis.

She saw two men sitting around a speakerphone. Their smiles were devious. Their eyes were filled with evil. Julie was drawn closer to the two men and their conversation. Still unable to be seen or felt, she listened in. Surprisingly, she recognized one of the men as the man she saw with April at Samantha's house.

She witnessed one of the two men press the hold button on the phone. He seemed to be in charge.

He said, "Listen, Mario. Be sure you tell him to cut the red wire. Let him believe this will disarm the bomb. You got that—the red wire. If he cuts the green, it's all over. The bomb will be rendered useless and will not detonate. He has to cut the red wire, understand?"

The man took the phone off hold. The individual named Mario spoke.

"Cut the red wire."

Julie heard the person on the other end of the phone confirm. "So the red wire, correct?"

Julie was horrified. They were talking to Steve! She had been at the bomb site when Steve was hovering over the bomb. She had heard this conversation over Steve's phone. These were the two men Steve was receiving instructions from.

The phone suddenly went dead. The men cheered as if they just won a championship game. They joked on how they duped Steve into cutting the wrong wire. *This can't be happening*, Julie thought. They had used Steve as a pawn. It had become clear to her that she was seeing events in reverse. She somehow had to stop this nightmare. She needed to stop Steve but how? No one could hear or see her. She wondered if she was too late. Maybe Steve was already dead.

The lights went dim on Julie. The scenario she had just witnessed faded to distant laughing. Soon she was back in darkness, hearing and seeing nothing.

Mario Continues His Plan

Mario had concocted a plan that he felt was foolproof. He went to the control room and made an announcement.

"Listen up, people. I want to find every bit of information on Steve Mitchell we can. Check the information we had on him before he crashed. Check every source you have. I want to know everything there is to know about this guy in thirty minutes. Now move it."

The workers in the control room furiously worked their computers. Every source was checked and every fact compiled in the thirty minutes Mario had given them.

Through the organization's connections, Mario had gathered all the information about Steve he needed. He knew where he lived, where his office was, and where he had his hangar. Literally, Steve's entire life history was at his disposal.

Mario went to one of the back-storage closets within the command center and wheeled out a wooden crate. It was the same one that was on Steve's plane when he crashed—the same one that contained the triggers and the gold Steve saw back in 1962 when he was facing the mob then.

How Mario ended up with it was a mystery. He wouldn't tell anyone how he laid his hands on it. But he had, and now it was going to work to his advantage.

He enlisted the help of one of the bodyguards to lift the empty crate into his SUV. Both men climbed in and left for the Saint Paul Airport. Mario was going to use the crate as a ploy to cast aspersions on Steve to Eddie that he really did steal the triggers. His plan was to then use this information as leverage against Steve to recover the gold from him.

Mario was devious. But more than devious, he was desperate. He did not want to face the wrath of Aziz should he fail in getting the gold back from Steve.

The men drove to the hangar where Steve kept his business aircraft stored. They turned the headlights off as they got closer. This was to be a covert operation. Around the back, there was an outside-storage container that Steve kept miscellaneous items of no value. It remained unlocked.

The two men quietly slipped from the vehicle and lifted the crate from inside. They opened the door to the storage container and placed it inside.

Both men returned to the vehicle and drove a quarter mile down the side street and parked so they had a clear view of the storage container. Mario called the command center and had a previously written anonymous e-mail sent to Eddie, giving the location of the crate on Steve's premises.

Just as Mario had expected, it wasn't long before a dark-colored vehicle drove up to the storage container. The person exited the vehicle, and Mario could see the flash of a camera inside the container.

Eddie, the Morretti crime boss, will now see firsthand where his crate that once contained bomb triggers had ended up. Steve was set up by Mario to appear as the perpetrator of taking the mob's property. Ironically, it was the same way Steve set up Billy and Luke back in 1962 with the same crate.

A Surprise Visit in Steve's Office

Steve was in his office early the next morning. There were so many moving parts to this entire saga that he needed to jot down his thoughts on what he had seen since the hospital stay a few days ago in Lake Tahoe.

Foremost on his mind was Julie. He worried about her welfare while she was being held captive by a gang of mobsters. It saddened him that he was unable to keep her out of harm's way. He even told her to stick close to him at the Pasta Palace and that she would be safe with him. Those words haunted Steve. He questioned how he could have done things differently so the outcome wasn't what it was. Steve also felt saddened by the loss of April. He thought, *Another instance of letting someone down,* but with April, it was the ultimate letdown. She died behind the wheel of his car. She never had a chance. She never even knew what hit her. Steve imagined her emotions as she drove away. They were probably of relief that she was finally away from Mario and that house of captivity.

Steve was being faced with some very hard decisions. He had hard choices to make, and none of them made sense. He had to make those choices without letting his emotions get in the way. Life was more difficult than he ever could have imagined. He had to piece together the puzzle of the last few days if he was going to be successful in rescuing Julie from her captors.

Steve picked up a scratch pad and drew a vertical line down the sheet of paper. On the left, he labeled "Things I can control," and on the right, he labeled "Things out of my control." He stared at the paper without writing anything else. After a few minutes, he ripped the piece of paper from the pad and crumpled it into a ball. He had one and only one goal in mind, and that was to rescue Julie.

Steve heard a car drive up to his office door. He heard three car doors slam and muffled speaking. He hurriedly left his desk and headed to the door to lock it. He did not want any uninvited guest to enter. It wasn't the time or the place.

Before he got halfway across the room, the door burst open. There stood Eddie and two of his bodyguards. He was slowly slapping a pair of leather gloves in his hand. His smirk told Steve that this was not a friendly visit.

Steve kept his composure as he said, "Listen, I didn't invite you in my office, and I don't appreciate you barging in like this."

Eddie was out of patience. Without saying a word, Eddie slapped the gloves hard against Steve's face. He then grabbed him by the shirt collar and threw Steve to the floor. Steve wiped the blood from his lip on his shirt sleeve. He was about to get up and fight back when Eddie motioned to his two thugs behind him with his finger to have his boys set Steve down. The two men acted immediately. They knew what the boss wanted. Each rushed at Steve, grabbing him by either arm and throwing him to the couch next to his desk. While Eddie's bodyguards held Steve in place on the couch, Eddie grasped Steve's chin with his big hand. He held Steve's face a mere inches from his as he spoke with a clenched mouth.

"Stevie, my boy, let's set the record straight. I don't need yours or anyone else's permission to walk in your office. You took my property, and I will get it back, and to get it back, I don't care if I have to kill you, your girl, or your mother."

Steve tried reasoning with Eddie one more time even though his jaw was firmly clasped between Eddie's fingers.

"Eddie, I told you I didn't take your crate. I was in the hospital, so how could I have it?"

Eddie let go of Steve's chin. Steve spat the blood in his mouth to the floor. Eddie retrieved an envelope from his coat pocket. From within the envelope, he pulled two photographs. He took the first photo and held it up to Steve's face so he could see it.

"Is this not a picture of your storage container just outside of your hangar?"

Steve just looked at the picture without saying anything, which enraged Eddie. He slammed his left fist against Steve's face, drawing even more blood.

"Well, is it?" Eddie sternly asked.

"Yeah, it's mine. So what?" Steve answered.

Eddie tossed the picture to the floor. He grabbed a second one from the envelope. He held this one closer to Steve than the first.

"Now, do you see that crate? Do you? Answer me!"

Steve could not believe his eyes. The wooden crate has reappeared in Steve's life yet again.

"Yes, I see it! What do you want me to do about it?" Steve sarcastically answered. He was tired of seeing this pesky crate. It seems to have brought Steve nothing but grief every time it shows up.

Eddie gave a backhand swipe across the right side of Steve's face.

"Here's an answer you can give me," Eddie shouted. "If you didn't take my property, how did I get a picture of the crate in your storage shed last night? Answer me that, *Mr. I Didn't Take Your Stuff.*"

Steve answered in disbelief, "My storage shed? Impossible, someone must have planted it."

Eddie threw this picture to the ground too. He gave one more blow to Steve's face and motioned to his boys to turn him loose. As the three walked out the door, Eddie sarcastically said, "The clock is ticking, my boy . . . tick, tock, tick, tock, tick, tock. It's time to do something, Mr. Mitchell."

Steve sat flabbergasted at seeing the pictures of the crate in his storage unit. As soon as he saw Eddie's car leaving the premises, he went to the bathroom to clean up his beaten face. Eddie had smacked him around pretty good.

Steve was still unsure how the crate ended up in his storage area. He knew it was planted, but by who was the question.

Steve decided he needed to see this for himself. He jumped in his vehicle and headed for the hangar where the storage shed was located. When he got there and opened the door, there it was. That same wooden crate that seems to be following him was sitting right in the middle of the floor. Now Steve was totally confused. This crate was continuing to bring grief to him.

Mario Makes His Move

A dark sedan drove up as Steve secured the door to the storage shed. He left the crate inside. The sedan's windows were tinted dark, so Steve could not see who it was. He knew it either had to be the feds or more of the bad guys. The car stopped next to Steve, and the rear window rolled down about an inch. The person in the backseat was talking to Steve.

In a monotone voice, the person spoke distinctly. "We know who you are. We know about the crate. We know about the gold, and we know that Eddie has your girl. If you care to see her alive, we need to talk. A meeting has been set for 3:00 PM today at the Old Town Street Side Café on Mounds Avenue and Highway 61 in Saint Paul. Come alone. It may just save your girl."

Before Steve could answer or even ask questions, the window rolled up, and the car drove away. Steve just shook his head in disbelief. As if he needed more to worry about. In the car, Mario asked his driver if he thought Steve would show for the meeting. The driver's thoughts were that yeah, he probably would. There was a lot riding on his girl.

That Afternoon at the Café

Steve arrived early at the café for the 3:00 PM meeting. He felt the need to scope out all the activity around the neighborhood eatery. It was a famous place with a lot of people coming and going. It was the perfect place to have a private meeting in a public forum. Everyone was too concerned with their own lives to worry about someone else's.

Steve sat outside at a table in the far corner away from the street traffic. The people in the car did not identify themselves and never left any instructions other than to meet at the café. Steve watched people come and go and wondered with each one whether it was the person that he was to meet.

At precisely 3:00 PM, a gentleman with shoulder-length hair and sunglasses walked up to Steve and sat down. Steve recognized him as the guy that was with April at her mom's house.

"I knew from the get-go that you were trouble for April," Steve said.

"Hey, easy, cowboy, this is going to be a friendly meeting. Deal?"

Steve just glared at him.

The man in the sunglasses continued. "My name is Mario, and I'm going to tell you something you don't know but you will want to listen to. I know I can be truthful with you because you won't and can't go to the authorities. The Morretti clan wants something, and you want something that they have. I believe her name is Julie.

"You see, Steve, my organization, as well as myself, has a bit of a vendetta to play out with your government. Too bad you crashed that night with your plane. It would have been so much easier on most people if you would have just made it to California. Do I have your attention now?"

Steve just answered, "Go on."

"I said most people because for us, it was a bit of a windfall. The Morrettis are known in the underworld for producing some really high-grade weaponry. It just so happened that that crate you were carrying had some very expensive triggers for a dirty bomb."

Mario paused for a moment and chuckled at Steve as he continued.

"Steve, you should see the look on your face. I bet you didn't expect that one, did you?"

Mario let out a slightly devious laugh. He continued relaying the story to Steve.

"We have some financers out on the West Coast that wanted to look at the actual product before plunking down a whole lot of cash. But you crashed, and that was that. Except our people were following you in a helicopter. They landed and grabbed the triggers from the crate before anyone showed.

"Oh yes, forgive my guys for not stopping to render aid during your most unfortunate accident. But they really didn't care. So now we have the triggers without paying for them. The Morrettis, well, they wanted to blame someone, and you were the closest to that ordeal. Now they think you have the triggers and are planning on fencing them. I do know without question they want them back and will stop at nothing to get them. I also think you believe they want the gold that you so daringly stole from me. You see, the Morrettis have no clue where the gold is unless you want me to tell them."

Mario chuckled while Steve was sitting at the table, taking it all in. He had a clear picture now on what had happened.

Mario continued. "I have a proposition for you. We don't have use for the triggers at this point. We didn't pay for them, so it's no big deal if we lose them. Besides, maybe we were a little bit overzealous on picking on your government. They have some wicked firepower that we probably don't want to get on the wrong side of. But we have other plans, and that gold you stole from me was going to be used for other necessary things.

"You need the triggers to get your girl back from the mob guys, and we need the gold. So here's what we are prepared to do. We trade even up. You get the triggers, and we take the gold."

Steve was in such a quandary. He was now mixed up with the mob, gold, and terrorist plots. *Which is the greater evil?* he thought.

Steve spoke up. "Let me see if I have this correct. You want me to give you the gold, and you'll give me the triggers so I can get Julie back. What prevents me from going to the Morrettis and telling them the truth about your little escapade with the triggers?"

Mario chuckled at Steve.

"By now I'm sure you've had contact with that wacko Eddie. Do you think you will get anywhere by telling him such a story? You know he has no leniency if he perceives you are lying. Do you want to take that chance? What I'm offering here is a compromise. You give and you get."

Mario had put an offer on the table for Steve, and once finished, he told Steve to think on it but to not think too long. He would get back to him for his decision in short order.

Mario got up from the table and gave one more bit of advice for Steve.

"If I were you, I wouldn't even think of contacting the authorities. If you do, there will be no one in your family that will be safe."

With that, Mario blended into the street traffic and was gone.

Steve Ponders This New Twist

Steve remained at the table. His dilemma had grown. He now realized that what he thought Eddie wanted wasn't at all found in the gold. He thought Steve had taken the bomb triggers, and that is what he was after.

He realized he had a tough choice to make. On one hand, Mario had a dangerous weapon of mass destruction. If he chose to use it, there was no telling how many lives would be lost. Steve only had the gold. It couldn't harm anyone, but it could be used to purchase massive terror campaigns.

Steve's thoughts jumbled together. He knew Mario was right. Going to Eddie was out of the question. Eddie bordered on the psychotic. In the end, Steve decided to play ball with Mario only to buy some time. He would find a way where the gold and the triggers were a lessened threat. By going along with the trade, it might just get Julie back safely and at the same time put some very hardened individuals behind bars for a long time.

Steve left the café for his office. He would wait for Mario to make his move and contact him. There was nothing more to do but wait.

Chapter 9

Mario and Aziz Meet

That evening, Mario got together with Aziz at a local pub so he could discuss his plan with him. They sat at a secluded table toward the back of the room. Mario was feeling confident that his plan would work. Aziz listened intently as Mario laid out his intentions.

"Aziz, I think I've got this figured out. Steve believes we are going to trade the triggers for the gold. But that is not going to happen. We're going to get the gold and blow him up with the triggers at the FDC Center. Then we'll have the gold, and our fight against the financial markets will have started."

Aziz chuckled at Mario's quick synopsis of his plan.

"Well, that sounds all dandy and fine, but I have some questions. How do you plan on blowing him up with the triggers?"

"I'm going to make a deal with him. We're going to do the trade, but to keep him honest, he's unknowingly going to have to dismantle the bomb to get the triggers. If they are attached to the bomb, he will have more motivation to trade the gold for the triggers. I'm sure he doesn't want innocent people to die, so he's going to accept the deal to save all those people.

"I've talked to our technicians on how to do this. They are going to set up the bomb so that if any wire is cut other than the one the timer is attached to, the bomb will detonate. The trigger has three wires to it: a red, blue, and green. I'm going to be on the phone, instructing him while he dismantles the trigger. If I tell him to cut the red wire and he follows my instruction, it's boom time. The bomb is strong enough to bring down the entire building, which will start our terror campaign."

Aziz questioned, "But if he cuts the green wire, nothing is going to happen. The bomb doesn't go off, and then we are done."

Mario smiled as he answered, "He won't know about it. I'm not going to tell him where he can find the trigger until the last minute. Steve will be so thrown off-balance on thinking about a bomb in a building that he won't be able to concentrate on an alternative plan."

Aziz thought for a minute on the plan Mario had just spelled out. It sounded to him that it might just work. If it did, Mario was right. The terrorist plan that he had been hoping to start would be off to a huge start. He had a couple of questions though. He wondered whether Mario could convince Steve to go along with trading the gold for the triggers, and if he did, was Steve good enough to get to the bomb in the FDC Center undetected?

Julie Visits a Strange Site

Julie was first aware of the sounds of traffic. She could hear numerous vehicles on the streets. The sounds of people and a water fountain soon joined the traffic. As her senses came to life, she found herself at the corner of Fifth and Forty-Second Street. She recognized she was on the edge of Bryant Park in New York City. *Why here?* she thought.

She walked from the corner into the park, passing by the street-side café. Although she could hear and see people, she still could not communicate with them. Her sense of touch was gone too. Her hand would pass right through objects and people. She was alone in her experience.

Julie continued up the walkway toward the fountain located in Bryant Park. She had no purpose to, but she felt compelled to walk in the direction she was going. The sound of the water from the fountain increased as she walked toward it. The New York Public Library loomed large in front of her. As she rounded the fountain, there sitting at a lone table was Steve.

He sat silently, looking at the library that was located across the grassy park. He would glance at the building and then make notes in a notepad. It was a strange sight to her. She could not figure out what he was doing. Steve was so far away from where he knew he saw her last. Her thought was *Why is he not trying to rescue me?*

Soon Steve closed his notebook and got up from the patio table where he was sitting. He walked down Forty-Second Street toward the library building's entrance. Once inside, he did not take time to view the displays along the walls. He walked directly to the stairs and went to the third floor. Along the way, he would pause and write in his notepad.

Upon arriving on the third floor, Steve observed everything while making numerous notes. He paused for some time in front of room number 320 entitled The Berg Collection Reading Room.

Julie followed Steve the entire time. She was trying to make sense as to what he was doing. She observed him sitting on the bench outside of room 320 for quite some time. The last thing she saw was Steve approaching a guard in the rotunda. Her senses were fading as he talked with the guard. She couldn't quite hear what was being said before things once again went dark. She heard nothing more and entered back into the void she had just come from.

A Master of Weaponry

Peter was employed in Aziz's terror group as the team's pyrotechnician. His extensive experience with bombs made him a valuable team member. His quest for the same terroristic endeavors as Aziz made him a perfect fit. Peter also excelled in the art of espionage.

Mario wanted to get his plan in action as soon as possible. He had met Peter before on several occasions. As it was with Aziz, the outlook of the two men was similar, and they hit it off almost immediately. Mario was confident he could count on Peter to come through if asked.

Mario knew his plan to get rid of Steve was going to have to be an intricate one. The dirty bomb would need to be placed in the FDC Center, which would be no easy task. The next thing he had to do was make sure Steve could get into the building and reach the bomb undetected. Neither feat was a walk in the park. Mario decided to test Steve's ability on a trial run before he sent him into the FDC Center.

Mario placed a call to Peter. He explained what the plan was and asked if Peter could set up the bomb and if he could test Steve's stealth ability. Both were of no problem to Peter. When asked, he was more than glad to take on the project, especially with the amount of gold the group stood to gain.

Peter told Mario that he would handle everything. He would test Steve's skills in a very special way—one that would not be an easy task. The stage was set for a showdown between Aziz's organization and Steve.

Peter Gets Busy

Peter didn't waste any time in getting started. His upstate New York home was secluded from the general public. It allowed him to operate undetected. He had the components of the dirty bomb, and all he needed was the trigger from Mario.

He boxed everything he would need separately. He made sure each was packaged generically so it would not raise suspicions during shipping. Peter dropped half of the packages at an overnight-shipping location. He took the remaining half to a separate shipping office. He was minimizing the possible connection with what he was shipping. Once he arrived in Minneapolis, he would assemble all the components together.

His next stop was in New York City. He had extensive connections that ran deep in the city. It was time to put a plan in place for Steve to follow so Aziz's organization could test Steve's skills.

It was close to 6:30 PM when Peter met the guard at the front door of New York City's main library. Bryant Park, directly connected to the library, was filling with its usual nightlife while the general public began exiting the library for the evening.

"Peter, I heard you were stopping by. Good to see you," the guard said.

Peter greeted him with small talk and smoothly slipped the guard five crisp $100 bills so as to not be detected by others. The guard took the money and quickly slipped it in his pocket. He welcomed Peter into the front lobby. They made a short stop in a room not far from the main entrance. The guard unlocked the door and went in where he flipped a few switches on the main library's surveillance panel. They exited the room, and the guard locked the door.

The two of them made small talk as they walked to the third floor. There were a few other guards they passed along the way, and each greeted the other with just a nod. Once on the third floor, they walked by the McGraw Rotunda to room number 320, which was located at the far corner of the building. The sign on the door read The Berg Collection Reading Room.

The room was closed to the general public and was only used for the purpose of research by professors and graduate students. Because of the sensitive and invaluable manuscripts the room housed, special permission had to be granted to entrants days before their actual visits.

The guard and Peter paused and waited outside the room as another guard strolled through the rotunda down the hall. The guard glanced at the surveillance camera located outside the door to make sure the red recording light was off. Even though he had turned the camera off downstairs in the surveillance room, he wanted to make sure it stayed off.

The guard told Peter, "When I open this door, you will have only sixty seconds before a secondary alarm system is triggered. That's one I cannot control unless I'm sitting at the desk. So get done what you need to and get out. I'll wait here for you."

Peter agreed as he pulled an envelope from his pocket. The guard unlocked the door and looked at the second hand on his watch.

"Sixty seconds. Now go," the guard told Peter.

Peter quickly entered the room. The air temperature was kept cool to protect the manuscripts from deterioration. The room had a smell of old paper. The documents it protected were priceless.

Peter knew the layout of the room and immediately went to the left of the door. In the far corner and at the base of one of the research desks was a cold-air return vent. He slipped the envelope through the slats of the vent and returned to the door. It was well under the sixty-second limit.

Peter walked out and told the guard, "Done. Let's go."

Both men walked back down the stairs to the first floor. The guard returned to the surveillance room and reactivated the camera for room number 320.

"All done," the guard said to Peter.

Peter smiled and told him to take his wife out for a nice dinner. He reminded him to follow the instructions he gave him regarding Steve's visit. The guard confirmed, and Peter left the library and headed for the airport. The next stop was Minneapolis.

Julie Hears Aziz and Mario Plotting

The music from the local band playing off to the corner is what Julie heard first. There were people milling around a pub with drinks in hand, laughing and joking. None seemed happy; they were merely whitewashing the cares of the day away.

Julie was drawn to Mario sitting in the corner at a table with another man. The other man was one she had seen earlier while on another one of her premonitions. She moved closer to listen to their conversation. Mario mentioned the other gentleman's name as Aziz.

They were talking about Steve. More confusing to her was that they were talking about Steve having gold. Julie wondered if he had found the gold he was looking for and where he found it.

Listening to the men talk shed new light on the perception Julie had already conceived. She soon discovered they were plotting against Steve. The more she listened, the more she realized Steve was the victim and had not turned to the wrong side of the law as she had previously thought. The two men were setting Steve up to be killed and for a price. It was for the gold.

Julie was now longing for a way to contact Steve. She needed to warn him. Everything she had tried to enter into the present world had failed. Her world seemed to be playing in the reverse of Steve's. She worried she would be stuck in this void of not being able to communicate.

By now Julie recognized the sign that her consciousness was fading. She tried to gather as much of the information they were discussing before she lapsed into darkness again. Her last thought was *These guys are evil.*

Steve Hears from Mario

Peter called Mario from the New York LaGuardia Airport. Mario was in the kitchen of the command center, getting a cup of coffee. He saw on his cell phone that it was Peter calling. He had been anticipating this call.

"Peter, do you have good news for us?" Mario asked.

"Yep, as planned, everything is set in New York. I sent the packages overnight, and you should see them tomorrow morning. I'm hopping on a flight right now to Minneapolis. I should be there in a few hours."

"Good. I'll get the message to Steve, and we will see just how good this boy is," Mario answered.

Mario left the kitchen and returned to his office. There he composed a note to Steve on a pad of paper. He wrote the instructions Steve needed to follow to make the deal. But the main purpose of this procedure was to see if Steve could actually sneak into a secure area.

He completed the note, ripped it from the pad, and sealed it in an envelope. On the outside of the envelope, he wrote Steve's office address. He called one of his men to his office and gave him the envelope and instructed him to deliver it in person.

After his man left, Mario leaned back in his chair and contemplated all that was going to take place. He knew that once this process started, it wasn't going to stop. In the end, Steve would be dead, a major Minneapolis financial icon would be destroyed, and Aziz's terrorist organization would have struck a major blow to the security of the United States.

Steve was at his desk when he heard a knock on his door. He hesitated to answer it. Last time someone came to his office, it was the unsavory character Eddie. He fought his reluctance and went to the door anyway.

He opened it to see a young man with an envelope in his hand.

"You Steve Mitchell?" the young man asked.

"Yes, who wants to know?"

Mario's courier did not answer. He just held out the envelope and said it was from Mario. Steve took the envelope, and the courier left.

Steve sat at his desk and opened the sealed envelope. He pulled out a single sheet of paper. It read,

Steve, if you are going to do this deal to save your girl from Eddie, here are your instructions. Since we hold the upper hand, we are going to require you to work a little for this. It's going to sound strange, but oh well, too bad. We want to make sure our interests are protected.

Your explicit instructions are not here in the Minneapolis area but rather in New York City. Go to the main library next to Bryant Park. Go to room number 320, the Berg Collection Reading Room. Inside the room and to the left of the door, there is a cold-air return vent of which you will find an envelope with specific instructions on what to do next. Retrieve that envelope, and we can do the deal.

Mario

Steve turned the paper over and back again. Nothing more was written. The instructions were perplexing. He thought, *Why New York? Why do this at all?* After thinking, he knew he had to do this for Julie. She was the victim here. But Steve knew it was not going to end the way Mario had planned. He would find a way to change that. He didn't know how at this point, but he was sure he would find a way.

Julie Comprehends the Gold

Julie's senses awoke in the passenger seat of a car. She looked around and saw nothing out of the ordinary. She tried to reason why she was there. Suddenly, the driver's door swung open. Julie was shocked to see Steve jump in. She so wanted to talk to him, but there continued to be no response to her tries.

Steve's forehead dripped with sweat, and he was breathing heavy as he started the car. A gunshot rang out and shattered the rear window, sending the bullet through the front seat and lodging it in the dash. A second shot shattered the rearview mirror off the driver's door. She looked to the rear of the car to see the muzzle of an automated weapon firing from the front door of the house behind them. There on the front steps stood Mario pointing at the car. Several men surrounded him, and all were firing automated weapons in Steve's direction.

Steve floored the accelerator and drove off at a high rate of speed. Julie watched as he wiped the sweat from his brow. He kept a keen eye behind him to see if someone was following.

After it was evident he had cleared the gunshots, Steve slowed the car down. She watched his demeanor as he drove. His forehead wrinkled often. His eyes had deep circles below them. The constant checking behind him made her realize just how much stress he had been under since her abduction.

Julie watched as Steve drove the car to his hangar. He stopped just outside the hangar door. Once he opened it, he drove the car inside and closed the door. She saw him open the trunk, and there it was—a trunk full of gold!

"Steve, you found it! Steve . . . Steve!"

No reaction came from him. She still could not communicate in any way. She watched him close the trunk as her senses began to fade once more. She entered the darkness as Steve was dialing someone on his phone.

Steve Goes to New York City

Steve took the next flight out to New York City. He was worried that the longer this entire ordeal went on, the more danger Julie would be subject to. Within a few hours, he would be at the New York Public Library to discover what he was up against.

During the flight, he read through the information he had downloaded from the Internet regarding the Berg Collection Reading Room. He discovered it was a locked and secured area. The general public could not just walk in to view its contents. Professors and graduate students actually had to submit requests days before stating what they intended to research in the room's manuscripts.

The plane was cleared for landing as Steve watched the Manhattan skyline whisk by. He was missing Julie like he had never missed anyone before. During the flight, he recalled so many things he enjoyed about her. Even though she was being held captive for a ransom by the Morrettis, Steve felt he could almost feel her presence at times over the last few days.

Once landed, Steve hailed a cab at the airport's curbside. He told the driver to take him to Bryant Park at Forty-Second and Fifth. The cab driver held a one-way conversation about the different concerts he had been to at the park over the years. Steve heard him talking, but it was just meaningless babble to him. He was more concerned as to what was ahead for him.

The driver stopped at the corner of Forty-Second and Fifth next to the street-side café at the park. Steve handed him $60 for a $40 fare. He told the driver thanks for the ride and closed the door to the taxi. The taxi maneuvered back into traffic and blended into the already-congested city streets.

Steve walked past the café and followed the path that led to the park. He sat at an outside table between the fountain and the manicured lawn. As people relaxed on the grass, Steve saw the New York Public Library looming large adjacent to the far side of the grassy area.

He observed many diverse people in the park. He thought about his dilemma and how different it must be from the carefree attitudes of those enjoying their open-air afternoon in a crowded city. But then, he thought, maybe not. No one knows what goes on deep within oneself. Feelings, conflicts, and safe havens are left to the individual.

The woman at the table next to him caught Steve's attention. She was an older lady that sat alone. He could see she had a newspaper tilted slightly upward as she read it. Every few minutes, she would stop and hold a conversation with an imaginary person. The woman would pause as if the imaginary person would be answering her questions.

What took Steve by surprise was that the woman was talking like a nuclear physicist. She was obviously brilliant yet misguided. He wondered where she came from and what disconnect took place in her life that brought her to the place she was in today.

Steve thought about what Jake had said during his prison interview with him. Jake had been reading about people that time travel, as rare as that may seem. Steve knew firsthand that it does happen. He had been in that situation twice now.

The old lady started the conversation again with her imaginary friend. Steve couldn't help but wonder if this was one of the people Jake had talked about. Could she have been a time traveler, and if so, had the experience taken her sanity from her? Steve worried about himself because of what he had experienced. Would he too someday end up in the park, talking to an imaginary friend? He had to quickly get out of this thought pattern. It disturbed him too much.

Steve took out a pad of paper. He sketched the library in relation to the streets. Although he was there to follow instructions from Mario's group for the gold trade, he still wanted to make sure he had an escape route should things go wrong. He made notes about every little thing.

He entered the library through the main entrance. Security was tight, but Steve quickly passed through the metal detectors. The guards were busy searching backpacks and laptop bags. He noticed a room off to the side that had its door open. A security guard was exiting the room. Inside he could see the many monitors and security arrangements the library had. He knew his task was not going to be easy.

He stopped the guard that was exiting the room to ask him what room the Berg Collection was in. Steve still had his sunglasses on and was looking into the room behind the guard as he spoke. He was making mental notes of what security systems may be employed by the library. He did notice there was only room for one guard at the desk to monitor the security screens.

Steve thanked the guard and headed up the main stairway to the third floor. The architecture of the library was magnificent, but he was not on a sightseeing tour. He was there to get his instructions and get out undetected. At the top of the stairs, he passed the McGraw Rotunda just outside of the Rose Reading Room. The Berg Collection Reading Room was straight ahead at the end of the hallway on the right in room number 320.

As Steve passed the different checkpoints where guards stood, he made notes on his pad of paper. When he got to the end of the hallway, he stood looking at the glass door to room number 320. Behind that door and to the left was the vent that contained the instructions for the gold exchange that Steve had traveled so far to retrieve.

A public bench was against the wall of the far side of the hallway across from the reading room. Steve sat down to observe the area and make a plan. He saw what was called the north stairway to his right that led directly down to a public side exit onto Forty-Second Street. Behind him and to the left was a shorter hallway that led to the public restrooms.

Steve could see the door to the reading room directly across from him. At the top of the door was a security camera monitoring whoever went in and out of that room. In the middle of the research room was a desk that an attendant sat at. All seemed quiet except for Steve's mind. He was observing every little detail that surrounded that room.

The attendant in the room got up from her desk and walked toward the exit. Once at the exit, she pressed a button on the doorjamb, unlocking the door for her to exit. She exited and Steve could hear the automatic lock engage as the door closed behind her. On the desk was a secondary LED light that went out as she exited to use the restroom. Steve watched that light, and in exactly sixty seconds, it lit up again.

The attendant returned after a few minutes and was quietly talking on her cell phone. It distracted her as she pressed the key code on the wall to reenter the room. She was so consumed with her conversation that she made no attempt to hide her fingers typing in the code. Steve quickly memorized the code: 560219.

He watched as the LED light on the desk went out when the door was opened, and exactly sixty seconds later, it came back on. Steve surmised that this was a secondary alarm or camera system inside the room and it must be activated by the door opening and closing. The woman did not stay long before she left the room again with a large stack of folders and headed downstairs. As far as Steve could tell, this left the room empty.

Steve got up from the bench and timed how long it would take him to go down the north stairway and exit onto Forty-Second Street. He then went back up to the bench and worked through a plan to get himself into that room.

He decided the outside-door camera was going to be a problem. It was constantly hot, showing every movement around the entry. Steve was going to have to create a diversion long enough to distract the guard monitoring the cameras downstairs in the security room to allow time for Steve to get in that room.

A young man, dressed with a statement to make against the establishment and carrying a backpack, walked past Steve on his way to the restroom. Here was his diversion. Steve waited for the man to leave the restroom and walk back toward the McGraw Rotunda. As the man entered the rotunda, Steve had a bit of luck. The man stopped and pulled out his cell phone and began texting.

Steve quickly pulled a guard aside and said, "I don't know if there is anything to it, but I overheard that man standing over there in the restroom in one of the stalls, talking to someone on the phone that he had enough explosives to bring down the roof of this place in his backpack. Probably nothing to it, but I had to say something."

The guard responded, "Really? We'll handle this right now."

Steve excused himself from the guard because he didn't want the man to recognize him as a snitch.

The guard said, "Not a problem. Go downstairs and see the guard in the security room."

The guard then called in a security breach to the guard downstairs and advised of the situation.

Within a few seconds, several guards had surrounded the poor man and had him on the floor spread-eagled. The diversion was working. The commotion in the rotunda was enough to divert the security room's attention away from the door of the reading room. Steve hurried down the hallway to room number 320. He pulled a ball cap from his pocket and put it on along with his sunglasses to disguise himself from any video recordings. He entered the code of 560219 and opened the door to the reading room.

Once inside, he began counting backward from sixty. He did not want to activate the secondary alarm. Steve quickly found the vent and undid the wing nuts holding it in place. When he pulled the vent free from the wall, there inside was the envelope he was looking for. He grabbed it and shoved it in his pocket.

He was down to eighteen seconds until the secondary alarm locked in placed. There was no time to replace the vent. Steve left it lying on the floor and bolted for the door. Once outside the room, he glanced down the hallway, and the young man he had set up was sitting cross-legged on the floor while the guards were examining the contents of his backpack.

Steve knew it would only be a matter of seconds before the all clear was sounded. He hoped the man with the backpack would forgive him for setting him up like that. Steve quickly retreated down the north stairway and exited onto Forty-Second Street. There he caught a bus to Union Station. He held the envelope in his pocket until he could safely read it.

The guard in the security room gave the all clear to the other guards, stating it was all a false alarm. The guard Steve had talked to in the rotunda relayed to the security room that Steve was on his way down there. He wanted to mention their gratitude for being a citizen who cared. He described Steve to him and told the security room that he did not have the time to catch the gentleman's name.

Once the guard in the room had a description of Steve, he went immediately to the monitor that overlooked room number 320. Peter had told him to be on the lookout for Steve. Sure enough, he should have been.

The guard looked at the monitor and said out loud, "Well I'll be."

Clearly on the monitor, the guard could see the vent lying on the floor. He picked up the phone and called Peter.

"Your guy is good. I mean really good. In and out, and I never saw him."

Peter just laughed at the guard's synopsis and said, "Great, that's what we need."

Steve disembarked the bus at Union Station. He found a public bench away from the hustle and bustle of the city life. There he pulled the envelope from his pocket. There were no markings on the outside. It was just a plain standard-sized envelope.

He ripped the end open and pulled out a single sheet of paper. Steve unfolded the paper and read.

Steve,

The good thing is, if you are reading this letter, that means you have safely retrieved it from the vent. The bad thing is, this is not your instructions.

You see, we had to test your sincerity. We knew if you truly wanted to make a deal, you would jump through this hoop. I must say you did a fine job too. We had a guard on the inside that was to watch you, and evidently, somehow you slipped by him. Nice work.

Now let's make this deal. I'll be in touch with you back in Minneapolis.

Mario

Steve crumpled the letter in anger and tossed it in the garbage. He was seething with irritation. Julie was in danger, and here this whack job was playing games. He was ready to get back to Minneapolis but needed to calm his nerves before meeting Mario, or he may do something really stupid.

Chapter 10

Julie Sees April

It was dark outside when Julie awoke in the woods. She had no clue what this was all about. She saw two people standing near the tree line and talking. She moved closer. It was April and Steve. April was whimpering while Steve attempted to console her and at the same time give her instructions.

Steve was talking to her about the gold and how it belonged to the mob and not her mother, Samantha. He warned her she had to hide for a while and that things would not be safe for her. She recognized in Steve a quality of genuine concern. She saw the love he had from his heart. It was not a relationship-type love but one that said he really did care for someone's well-being.

She observed April's tearful gratitude for Steve's help. She saw her genuine remorse for leaving Steve back in Hawaii. After a hug and kiss of gratitude, she followed April to Steve's car. Julie sat in the passenger seat, watching April as she started the car, pushed the home button on the GPS, and drove off. During the next thirty seconds, she watched the relief on April's face from the nightmare that had just ended and a look of hope take over her facial expressions.

April was smiling when the car bomb went off. Julie knew she never had a chance as she watched the car being demolished all around her by the bomb. It only took a moment for April to lose her life as Julie watched it happen. The smile April had never faded as her heart stopped beating.

Julie found herself back in the woods with Steve. She could see the horrible shock on Steve's face as he watched his car and April disappear in a ball of flames and tangled metal. She watched Steve slump to the ground in tears. The compassion he had caused Julie to love him all the more.

Suddenly, Steve sprang to life and dashed through the woods. Julie could barely keep up with him. He rounded the corner of the old house and headed straight to the car.

As he leaped in the driver's seat and drove off, guns blazed from the house. Julie realized she had seen this play out once before. Before her world went black again, she realized this was the scene with her riding in a car with Steve as the back window and driver's mirror were shot off. More importantly, she remembered it as the car that contained the gold.

Mario Lays Out His Plan to Steve

Steve returned to Minneapolis from the wild-goose chase he had been on in New York City. In Steve's mind, he did not have to be tested. He was totally focused on saving Julie from the criminals that held her.

Steve retrieved his luggage and left the terminal and walked to his car in the parking lot. He placed his luggage in the backseat and drove off to his office. He did not notice the black SUV following him. It kept a distance from Steve but was following nonetheless.

At the office, Steve nervously paced as he waited for some sort of contact from Mario. There was nothing he could do until an exchange location was identified. He felt helpless and alone. Too much time had elapsed for his liking. He had not had contact with Julie for way too long. It made him nervous.

The knock on the office door was swift and hard. Steve did not hesitate to open it. He was anticipating contact from Mario. He opened the door, and there stood the man that quickly had become a thorn in Steve's side.

"You're a real piece, you know that, Mario? Your little New York stunt cost me time, and if it cost me Julie, well, you couldn't run far enough or fast enough."

Mario got in Steve's face.

"Listen, Mr. Steve Mitchell, don't you threaten me! In case you don't understand, I lost someone in this deal already. April may have left you, but she was with me, and now she's gone. So get off your high horse before I just walk away and let Eddie do what he wants with you. Understand, hotshot?"

Steve brushed aside Mario's aggressive advances. He moved to the window and leaned on the wall and looked out as he spoke.

"Okay, what do you want? Let's get it done right now. I'm not waiting."

Mario was adjusting his shirt from the scuffle he had with Steve as he spoke.

"I knew you would not make it an easy exchange. I don't trust that you would not double-cross me. You want the triggers to get your girl, and I want the gold. There is no easy exchange. You're not going to hand over the gold without having the triggers in exchange, and I'm not going to hand over the triggers unless my hands are on that gold.

"So since I have the upper hand here, I'm going to give you another incentive to do the right thing. You see there was a reason I had to make sure you could get into the New York library without getting caught because you're going to have to do it again to get the triggers."

Mario walked over to Steve's trophy case. With his finger, he gently pushed the carving of Steve's Cessna 310 that he did back in the 1860s around on the shelf. He turned to Steve and continued with his plan.

"At 10:45 PM tonight, you are going to park your vehicle with the gold in it at the corner of Nicollet Mall and Seventh Street in downtown Minneapolis. It will be right by the FDC Center. We'll take the gold, and you will take the triggers. Except the triggers will be hooked to a dirty bomb in the subbasement of the FDC Center, and you will disarm the bomb to get the triggers."

Steve was aghast at what Mario just proposed.

"What! Are you kidding me? You are going to put the entire city in jeopardy for this gold? That's preposterous."

Mario answered Steve, "Ridiculous as it may seem, it's the only way I can assure myself that you will not double-cross me. I'll call you on your cell phone at 9:30 PM and give you directions on how to disarm the bomb and take the triggers. Easy enough, you get the triggers to get your girl back, and I get the gold."

Steve asked, "What's my assurance you will tell me how to disarm the bomb?"

Mario headed for the door as he answered, "Simple, Steve. You got to trust me. If I don't call you to give the instructions to disarm the bomb, I'm sure you will figure it out. You wouldn't want to blow up the city now, would you?"

Mario laughed as he headed out the door. Steve slammed the door shut after he left. He tried to reason what would happen if he didn't drop the gold as Mario had instructed. There was no alternative; he had to drop the gold. Steve couldn't put the entire city's population at risk of a nuclear explosion from a dirty bomb. There was no guarantee Mario's clan wouldn't blow the bomb remotely if the gold wasn't dropped.

Steve looked at his watch. It read 1:55 PM. He had a little over nine hours to pull this all together and figure out a way where he would be able to get into the FDC Center after-hours. He knew his first stop was to go get the gold from Terry.

Steve Retrieves the Gold

Steve called Terry to make sure he was home. He told him he would be over within the hour to pick up the gold he had hidden there and to meet him at the hangar. He quickly got off the phone and headed to Terry's place.

Terry was at the hangar, waiting to greet Steve. He was concerned for him. He thought whatever Steve was involved with couldn't be good. He saw the demeanor of his friend change in such a short time.

Steve backed his vehicle, a late-model dark-colored SUV, up to Terry's hangar. He wasn't going to be long. His timeline was short.

"Level with me, what's going on?" he asked Steve.

"Terry, I wish I could, but trust me, this is my fight. I know you care. I get that, but this runs so deep that I can't take a chance on bringing in any outsiders to solve this. By 11:15 PM tonight, it will all be over, and I will fill you in on every detail."

"Come on, Steve! Look at what we've been through together. I can help with whatever you're involved with. Don't do it alone. Let me in."

Steve just shook his head to say no. The two men silently loaded the gold without speaking. Steve was nervous for the evening, and Terry was hurt that Steve would not trust him to help.

They finished loading the gold. Steve covered it with a heavy black blanket to keep it from being seen. He closed the back of the SUV and turned to Terry.

"Listen, I see the hurt in your face about this whole ordeal. There is no doubt in my mind that you could overcome what I'm facing, but the stakes are too high for me to chance it. There will come a day, Terry. I promise . . . there will come a day."

"I hope so. I truly do hope so. Hang tough, Steve."

The two men shook hands, and Steve drove off. He was headed for the FDC Center to scope out his plan for that night's showdown. Steve hoped to have Julie back in his arms within twenty-four hours.

Mario and Peter Make Plans

Upon leaving Steve's office, Mario called Peter and told him it was time to visit the FDC Center with the goods. He told him to meet him back at the command center first. Mario needed to go over the plans to make sure he had everything correct for triggering the bomb.

On the way to the command center in Anoka, Mario thought of his actions. He knew perhaps hundreds would be killed that night when the bomb went off. The shock waves of another terror attack on the United States should send the markets crashing.

Mario's hope was to create a big-enough impact on the first strike to induce the financial collapse that Aziz and he had planned. Without it, they both knew subsequent attacks would have to be much more elaborate.

The false sense of security the American people were drawn into since the last attack in 2001 had created this opportunity. Once Minneapolis has been rocked with the powerful bomb, the US security forces will once again be heightened to its highest level, creating a difficult situation for Aziz and Mario to continue their reign of terror. That did not detour Mario's intentions. He was confident they could overcome any obstacle. He had spent so many years of self-indulgence into greed that his heart had hardened to the pain this plan was about to inflict on innocent lives.

Mario, Aziz, and Peter met in one of the back rooms of the command center. Peter had the bomb components assembled in place, waiting for the triggers. Mario brought the triggers needed to explode the bomb into the room with him. These were the very triggers Steve unknowingly was flying to California a few months earlier when he crashed in his Cessna 310. They were the same triggers owned by the Morretti crime organization that Aziz's and his group had stolen from.

Peter mockingly placed the first trigger between the first and second canister. This trigger would be hidden and not seen by Steve. He explained that this was the first step to creating an explosion that was much bigger than a normal bomb. This trigger brought nuclear infusion into the equation.

The second trigger was the one Steve would be working with. This was the trigger that would initiate the nuclear reaction in the trigger between the two canisters. He placed it on top of the housing that would contain the mechanism. The red, blue, and green wires were readily visible. He explained that the green wire was connected to a timer as a fail-safe mechanism to explode the bomb. Should Steve not show up as planned to trigger the bomb, at least they would be able to go ahead with their plans. Peter went on to explain that cutting the red or blue wires would immediately detonate the bomb. Peter emphasized that Steve had to cut either the red or blue wire. Cutting the green would totally disarm the bomb.

Mario and Aziz had their instructions clear for when Steve called. They would direct him to his death and the start of what they both had hoped would be another blow to the American economy. Peter left with the bomb components for the FDC Center. There, he would easily slip into the building and plant the bomb in the subbasement. Peter's espionage capabilities were stellar, leaving no structure safe from his abilities.

Steve Plans His Entry

Steve pulled his SUV into the parking garage at the FDC Center. He parked in a corner away from the main foot traffic. He had a lot of gold hidden underneath the blanket in the back of the vehicle, and he didn't want to take any chances on anyone seeing the contents. The gold was his bargaining chip to get Julie back from the Morrettis.

Steve sat for a little bit in his vehicle, watching the traffic move in and out of the parking garage. He knew he was dealing with some evil people and wanted to make sure he was not being followed. After several minutes, the parking garage seemed to contain only those that had a reason for being there.

Walking across the parking lot, Steve was keenly aware of his surroundings. He was concerned that he was being watched. He entered the elevator to the lobby. He thought about the people that shared the tiny area with him. Each had their own lives and different challenges they faced. Chances are they were not facing what Steve was facing, but they each had their own battles and their own pains.

The elevator opened up into an expansive lobby area. Steve found a public seat opposite of the elevator. From there, he watched the security guards' movements for over an hour. As he did with the security cameras at the New York library, he observed the routines of the guards. He knew most of all security systems, no matter the intentions, when it involved people, they would eventually become methodic with their movements.

There were two guards that covered the main floors. Each would trade places every twenty minutes. One would sit behind the desk while the other would do a door check. True to form, the guards had worked themselves into a routine that could be timed like clockwork.

After some time, Steve had his plan set for that evening. As he walked across the lobby for the elevator, he thought of Julie. Soon he would be able to get her back from the Morrettis. Then he would have to figure out a way to bring both the Aziz group and the Morrettis down. Although he was going to make a deal that seemed to be made with the devil, he was not going to let it be the end of it. He would find a way to stop them.

Julie Observes the Beginning

Immediately as Julie's vision lightened to where she could recognize her surroundings, she made no mistake on where she was. It was an office with a man sitting behind a desk, smoking a partially soggy cigar. He was a stern man that ruled his way and his way only. It was Eddie, the Morretti crime boss.

Standing over the desk was the love of her life, Steve. He was busy making a stand of his own. He was making it known that if one hair was harmed on Julie's head that Steve would seek him out and make him pay.

It was at that moment she realized the scene was right after the Morrettis had grabbed her and taken her to the back room by two of Morretti's men. She saw the desire in his eyes to protect her. She knew he loved her deeply by the stand he was taking against Eddie and his actions.

Julie thought about the experiences she has had since being abducted. She had seen so much. Destruction, secret meetings, Steve in New York, and worst of all, she saw Steve get killed by a massive bomb. Then it struck her as to what it all meant.

Julie was seeing Steve's actions after her abduction in reverse! He was trying to save her, and Mario was setting him up to be killed. Steve had no clue on what was to come, but Julie had seen it unfold from the ending backward.

She wondered how she would be able to stop all this from happening. Steve was barreling headlong into a trap. It was a trap that would certainly cause not only his death but the death of so many more.

Julie ran to Steve as he stood his ground with Eddie. She cried to him to stop. She followed him out the room to his car. She continually cried out to him so he would hear her. She reached out to touch him, but it was of no use. Her hands would go right through him. She needed to warn Steve on what was going to happen.

Julie's vision was fading. She fought it. She did not want to leave this place. She had not been able to gain Steve's attention. He was oblivious to her being there. Her vision faded; her sense of hearing went silent, and once more, Julie was plunged into a void of nothingness.

Steve Makes His Move

The clock showed 9:28 PM. Steve had an hour and a half to get what needed to be done to save Julie. He did not like the idea of the gold falling into the hands of Mario and his group nor did he like the idea of the bomb triggers ending up in the hands of the Morretti crime family. But he didn't have a choice right now. He had to do it to save Julie. Once she was safe, he would find a way to bring down both Mario and the Morrettis.

At precisely 9:30 PM, Steve's cell phone rang. He knew it would be Mario.

Steve answered the phone by simply saying, "Yes."

Mario answered back, "Okay, drive your vehicle to the corner of Nicollet Mall and Seventh Street. Park in the taxi stand, and wait for my man to come by. He will have a map of where the bomb is located. Once he verifies that the gold is in your vehicle, he will give you the map. From there, it's up to you on what you do."

Steve asked Mario, "How do I know what you are telling me is true?"

"You don't, but look, what do you stand to lose? If you do nothing, innocent people will die, and their blood will be on your hands. So, Steve, I would suggest you follow the instructions my man will be giving you."

Steve hesitated for a moment, perplexed at what he was facing. He still couldn't see any way out of this situation. He had to do what he was told, or hundreds of innocent people would die. His only option was to look for a way during this process to stop the madness.

Steve finally answered Mario. "Okay, I'll be there with the gold. I'm leaving now."

Mario hung up the phone and turned to Aziz. He told him that the plan was underway and that soon they would have the gold back in their hands and the terrorist plot would be engaged.

Steve left his office with the gold in the back of his SUV. This was it. He was committed to following this through. As he drove down I-94 through the Mid Cities area toward downtown Minneapolis, his thoughts were scattered. On one hand, he was trying to keep his wits about him to stay on track. But what loomed large in his mind was that he had the lives of so many people in his hand. If he failed, they would die.

On the other hand, he was trying to figure out how he could thwart the plans of Mario and the Morretti family. He wanted these thugs to pay for the pain they had inflicted on so many people. April's death would not be in vain. He would find a way to avenge that travesty.

Steve exited the interstate into downtown Minneapolis. The sky was illuminated with the reflecting lights of so many buildings. Straight ahead, Steve saw the bluish glow of the FDC Center towering over all the other buildings. It was the tallest structure in the area. It housed numerous banking and stock-trading facilities.

The time was 10:22 PM when Steve's SUV came to a halt in the taxi stand at Nicollet Mall and Seventh Street. The area was void of most traffic due to the late hour. Steve put his vehicle in park and waited. He waited for what seemed like an eternity, but in reality, it was just a few mere minutes. His palms began to sweat as he nervously looked for Mario's contact to show.

A knock on the passenger window startled Steve. He pressed the button to lower the passenger window, revealing a man in his late forties and dressed in black. He motioned for Steve to exit the car. As he did, the man nervously looked in all directions.

"Show me the stuff," he grunted.

Steve walked to the back of the SUV and raised the rear hatch. The man lifted each corner of the blanket Steve had for covering the gold. Each lift revealed a gleam from the gold.

The man asked for the keys to the vehicle and Steve obliged. Mario's man then handed Steve a half-folded sheet of paper along with a black bag of tools. As Steve stood on the sidewalk, unfolding the piece of paper that contained his instructions, Mario's man drove off in Steve's vehicle. Several seconds later, a second black SUV sped past Steve in the direction of Steve's vehicle, traveling at a high rate of speed.

Steve looked at the typed instructions given to him by Mario's messenger. The instructions were simple. It read,

> Enter the main lobby, and inform the guard you are here to record the hour-meter readings from the generators on basement level one. He will allow you to pass without question and will return to tuning in to his portable television. Take the south elevator to BB1, and exit to the right. Follow the zigzag and then turn right down the long corridor labeled with a red sign that will say Authorized Personnel Only. Take this past the second generator on the left. Between the second and third machines, you will find two canisters connected by a series of wires and boxes. Your mission is to disarm the bomb. Mario's cell phone number is listed at the bottom of this note. Call him when you are at the bomb location, and he will give you instructions for disabling the trigger device.

Steve picked up the small tool kit given to him by Mario's man and headed across the street to the main lobby of the FDC Center. Just as the note said, Steve informed the guard that he was there to read the meters. The guard instructed him to the south elevators and went back to adjusting his portable television. He did not check any form of ID or credentials. Steve concluded that the guard had taken a payoff.

He walked across the lobby and entered the elevator. He pushed the button labeled BB1 for the basement floor. As the elevator descended, he thought of his decision to go at it alone on this. Maybe it would have been a good idea to bring Terry in on this. After all, he did work as an undercover agent for the area. He may have been able to help.

The elevator door opened, and Steve exited as his note explained. The directions were fairly accurate. Soon he found himself in the long corridor that was leading to the location of the bomb. The red sign above read Authorized Personnel Only. The whine of the generators masked any nearby sounds. Steve passed the low-lying pipes, wires, and lights. Once he passed the second generator's location, he looked to find where the bomb was planted. He saw the canisters just as Mario had said. In between the two canisters were the wires and housing boxes that contained the elusive triggers.

Steve stared at the bomb menacingly. This was the culprit of so much grief that he had experienced. Now he had no choice but to follow through.

Steve placed his tools on the floor. He took his cell phone and dialed Mario's number. After Mario answered, Steve initiated the speakerphone on his cell phone. He listened intently as Mario began telling him how to supposedly disarm the bomb.

Julie Faces Her Biggest Challenge

Once again, clarity invaded Julie's sight. The sound of a hustling city was the backdrop to what her senses were beginning to focus on. Her first vision was that of the street signs of Nicollet Mall and Seventh Street. Across the street, she saw a familiar sight. It was the FDC Center, and the clock read 10:55 PM. This was the same thing she saw in her previous premonition—the very one where she witnessed the bomb explode right underneath Steve, bringing the FDC Center crashing down around her.

Her thoughts were confused as to why she was in this same spot again. *Have I returned for a purpose?* was the question she was asking herself. She thought that maybe this time she could stop Steve from making a terrible mistake. There was no time; she had to try.

Julie raced across the street to the FDC Center just as she had done before. This time, rather than stopping in the lobby, she ran right past the guard that was getting a drink at the water fountain. She knew he didn't see her anyway.

The doors to the elevator opened as they had before. The elevator took her down to the subbasement where Steve was. She ran through the maze of machinery, lights, and low-slung piping.

As she got closer to the second generator, she could hear the phone conversation as before. It became louder as she got closer. There in front of her was the figure of a man slumped over the bomb. It was Steve.

183

Julie began to yell, "Steve! Steve! Can you hear me? Please, Steve, stop what you are doing. They are trying to kill you."

Steve did not respond to Julie's pleading. She tried and tried to contact him. Each time, her words went unanswered. Her touch was not felt, and she would pass through him as if he was not there.

Her heart was crushed. She knew the outcome that was about to take place, but there seemed to be nothing she could do to stop it. There just wasn't any way to communicate with Steve. He continued working toward his death.

Julie finally turned away from Steve and walked down the long corridor, totally defeated. She couldn't fathom watching him die again. She passed by the first generator and slumped to her knees, crying. She realized she was about to fail at saving Steve and many other lives too. She knew the devastating plan Mario and Aziz had put in place was about to be a reality.

The things she had seen since her abduction had been numerous, but she couldn't make contact with anyone. She saw the entire plan of Mario and the Morrettis in reverse, and now she was back at the ending again, anticipating the building falling down around her at any moment.

As she was on her knees, sobbing, she ran her hands down her thighs. There it was, and she felt it for the first time. It was a round lump in her pocket. She reached in and pulled out the object.

"The Cal Neva coin!" she yelled to herself.

There in her hand was the illustrious coin Steve tossed to her when they searched for the long lost gold hidden in the backwoods of California. He told her at that time to hang on to it as it may just bring them luck at some point.

She said aloud, "I have not come this far to fail."

Julie wrapped the coin in her hand, stood up, and turned to face Steve one more time. After so many frustrating moments of not being able to touch things, it felt good to once again be able to feel an object. She clinched the coin harder and harder as she started to run toward Steve. The faster she ran, the more confidence she had that she would break through this time. She felt that the coin in her hand was the omen that would change her seemingly noncommunicative world.

Steve had the wire cutters in hand with the blades wrapped around the red wire. He was just starting to squeeze the wire cutter handles when something magical happened at that moment. Once again, a cosmic collision of time transported Julie back into reality. The moment of her impact into Steve was hard enough to knock them both to the floor.

Steve, startled by the sudden hit, looked at Julie in disbelief.

"Julie . . . Julie? Where did you come from?"

She was so happy to finally hear his voice say her name, but she knew explanations would have to come later. She picked herself up off the floor and went to Steve's phone, grabbed it, and threw it to the ground, shattering it into pieces, breaking the communication with Mario. She then turned to Steve.

"No time to explain, Steve. Just do as I say."

Steve, still in disbelief, just said, "What?"

Julie picked up the wire cutters from the floor and handed them to Steve.

"Don't question me," she sternly said. "Take these cutters, and cut the green wire, not the red. Do it now!"

Steve, still not sure on what was going on, said, "But that will—"

Julie cut him off in midsentence.

"Just do it!"

Steve looked at the wire cutters and then Julie. So many thoughts were going through his mind. He knew he was told by Mario that cutting the green wire would immediately detonate the bomb. But he had to listen to his inner voice and do what Julie had said.

He took the wire cutters, and without hesitation, he snipped the green wire as Julie instructed. Both stood silently, waiting to see what would happen. Nothing did. Steve had successfully killed the triggers for the bomb.

With his back, he slid down the side of the canister into a sitting position and wept. The pressure of all he had been through the last couple of days had boiled over to the breaking point. Julie held him and let him sob. She too had tears.

Finally, the two of them talked.

"Julie, how did you get down here, and where have you been for the last couple of days?"

Julie went on to explain how she was transported into the future from the back room of the Pasta

Palace. From there, she started seeing visions of what Steve was going through but only that she saw them in reverse. She told Steve of how she was unable to touch or speak to anyone. That was until the moment she felt the Cal Neva coin in her pocket. Both agreed the coin would have to go on the shelf in Steve's office next to the 1860s carving of his airplane.

Conclusion

Before they could continue much more with their conversation, they heard numerous footsteps running down the corridor from either side. All were dressed in police SWAT clothing and equipment. Leading one of the groups was Steve's best friend, Terry.

When he reached Steve and Julie, he gave the command to the other SWAT officers to stand down. He was quite shocked to see Julie standing with Steve.

"Steve, I am so glad you are okay. We tried to get here before you even got to the bomb, but the guard upstairs delayed us for a minute or two."

Steve was dumbfounded at seeing Terry and his team.

"How did you even know I was here?" he asked Terry.

"Well, there are a couple of things you need to know. First, we have had a two-year sting operation going on with the Morrettis. We suspected them of arms dealing but just couldn't get enough evidence to bring them down. With the bomb you handed us tonight, we will make sure they are put away for a long time. In fact, at this moment, the Pasta Palace is being raided, and we are rounding up all the players.

"Now the Aziz group was a little different story. We had no idea there was a terroristic sleeper cell operating in the area. You helped us on that."

Steve asked, "How did I help you with them?"

"Sorry, Steve, but after your first visit with me, I became concerned. So we bugged your office. Even though I vouched for you, my team needed to confirm you were not sympathetic to the Morrettis. So when our bug picked up your conversation with Eddie and then later Mario, we knew we had two fronts to attack on. We decided to watch and observe to gather as much intelligence as possible before making our move. It worked and worked well. That fortified command center up there by the Anoka Airport is simultaneously being raided as with the Pasta Palace. Hold on a minute."

A radio call was just coming in from Anoka. Terry listened for a moment, then acknowledged the call. He turned back to Steve and continued.

"Well, just got word that Mario and Aziz have been taken into custody without incident. I would say it has been a good night for law enforcement and one terrible night for the bad guys."

Steve said, "Sounds like it, but someone is having a real good time with the gold they took from the back of my vehicle."

"Maybe not," Terry said. "When you came to my place to store that gold, I knew something was not right. You were acting all weird on me. I wasn't going to let you get away with that. I placed a tracking device with the gold. Did you notice a dark-colored vehicle speed by right after Mario's man took your vehicle? Well, that was our guys on their way to take down your vehicle. Oh, and your vehicle and gold are fine."

Terry turned to Julie and asked, "And you, little lady, how did you get down here before us?"

Julie was about to answer when Steve interrupted her.

"Terry, I never knew you were watching me this whole time. Since you were, I think you can see I was one of the good guys. But there are some things you couldn't see. I'm not going to get into that here, but we will sit down, and I will tell you everything."

Steve turned to Julie and winked at her as he said, "And I do mean everything. We both have been blessed with an extraordinary gift, and we are going to learn how to manage that gift so it can be used for a good cause. Someday I hope to understand how we were chosen for this, but for today, I just want to get out of this basement."

Julie and Steve walked out hand in hand, talking about what was next. Was this the end to their adventures in time-dimensional travel, or have they just begun?

The End